WITCH GONE DRAGON

A Witchy Urban Fantasy Mystery

Maaja Wentz

Loon Lake

Book Cover design by Maaja Wentz

First edition 2025

Issued in paper and electronic formats.

ISBN 978-1-0694075-0-4

ISBN 978-1-7776864-9-9 (ebook)

1

On a cold December Monday, Tonya stood six stories off the ground wearing slippers, her white tresses dancing on icy gusts.

How did I get here?

Signs on the Mackenzie Residence rooftop forbade student access, but she was fighting a rebellion of the mind. With her toes on the edge of the building, she trembled, struggling to suppress the mounting needs of the tyrant sharing her head.

Deep breath. Think of something else, anything but flying.

She glanced back over her beloved city surrounded by woods and cornfields. These should be happy times. City Council had lifted the memory curse on her friends, and National Council had ruled that her settling of Jack Waldock wasn't murder. For one glorious day, Tonya had united the anti-magic Pure faction, pro-magic Mod faction, and the hide-magic Trad faction to replant trees in the cemetery. But this precious peace had exacted a deep cost and saddled her with a parasite she couldn't escape.

Jump! Jump! his reptilian voice rasped inside her head.

Shut up, Hatch! But the urge mounted, and she stared over Lakeshore Drive at water which was too distant to break her fall. To her right, the western end of Loon Lake narrowed to a river. Two miles ahead, tiny whitecaps curled near Grand Island at the center of the lake. Like a pig in a python, the roundish body of water narrowed on the eastern end to slither through the forests and farmland surrounding the modest city of Loon Lake.

Stop staring at the water and relax, Hatch crooned. *Leave the dirt behind and fly like a god.*

Since July, Hatch, the dragon hatchling, had invaded her mind and tried to commandeer her body, ordering her to surrender like an abusive boyfriend.

Don't you want to fly?

You mean fall.

Human, if you die, I do, too.

That's Tonya, not Human, she insisted. He'd enslave her mind at the first sign of weakness, transform her body, and steal her humanity—forever. Every time she refused to change, he came back with new arguments, invading her thoughts in the middle of the night.

Hatch stalked like a tiger, watching for weakness, ready to spring. Last week, he took her by surprise, seized control of one leg, and sent her tumbling down the stairs. Bruises and circles under her eyes drew early morning remarks in the cafeteria until Tonya covered them with makeup. Nothing would go her way until she could free herself from Hatch and the iron grip of her suffocating hometown.

Mayor Donna Ashton hated Tonya. The mother who raised Tonya shunned her, and Old Family folk distrusted her birth mother, Helen. Tonya was fighting for her life against a unique magical creature, but her family history meant she could expect zero sympathy. Loon Lake's ruling families would probably take Hatch's side over hers.

Yes, I'm the victim here.

If you're the victim, how come you made me sleepwalk up to the roof? I'm the one getting hypothermia. Dawn breezes cut through her pajamas, and she tried to step back from the roof's edge, but Hatch stopped her.

Near shore, flickering lights gathered and grew in a display visible only to practitioners of magic and cursed creatures like Hatch.

Hey! Who are you calling cursed?

Sorry. I meant to say scheming, manipulative, and lacking in any redeeming qualities.

While they bickered, a white structure rose, sending waves rippling across the lake. The vision grew clearer and brighter as it rose until the top deck of a sparkling cruise ship towered fifteen stories over the public pier. Tonya had never taken a cruise, but she liked to visit travel websites and drool over cruises and beach vacations. The minute she learned to control her powers, and rid herself of Hatch, she wanted to try big city life. Her university friends were from Toronto, real friends like Drake, Zain, and Priya, who never made her feel small.

Compared to the modest lake, the mid-sized cruise ship looked huge. It would be run by seven or eight hundred crew members trained to pamper a thousand vacationers in its restaurants, bars, hot tubs, and theater. Tonya stared, mesmerized, as tourists loaded into fifteen-foot boats hanging from the side.

Hatch exclaimed, *Flyby! Let's gooo!*

Calm down. When Hatch got agitated, Tonya's whole body tickled. Rubbing her arms didn't help, because the irritation came from the inside. *It's not like you've never seen it before.*

The cruise ship, sighted occasionally in the summer and weekly in the fall, appeared daily as the holiday season approached.

Mayor Ashton had walled off Loon Lake Village from Mundanes and reversed the law against magic use within its confines. This December, gangs of day-trippers packed the streets, joyful to cast spells, crowd taverns, and overrun stores unhindered by Mundane or magical laws. Overnight, Loon Lakers from the magical Old Families competed for space on the cobbled streets as gangs of spell-casting tourists raided precious Victorian Loon Lake Village.

Struggling to control Hatch, who threatened to hurt her or her friends when she refused to be bullied, Tonya wanted to join the carefree tourists and take Hatch to whatever far-flung lands the cruise ship disappeared to every morning at 3:00 AM. But if she couldn't do that, maybe she could tame him.

Let me off this roof, or I'll suck the life energy out of you.

Babe, I get stronger every day, and you can't kill me without killing yourself.

I am not your babe.

His snicker roared inside her head.

During the summer, Tonya had stopped a rampaging dragon who laid eggs inside the bodies of innocent swimmers. Before the hatchlings could devour their hosts, Tonya stilled the eggs.

Murderer!

I was forced to choose the people or the eggs.

Wrong choice, idiot! People are worthless. Dragons are rare, magical creatures.

The female dragon had also cut Tonya's abdomen to create an edible nest for her young. Tonya was trying to save herself when Donna Ashton used the Staff of Storms to steal Tonya's powers and channel them into the egg, speeding its development until it hatched.

With his teeth gnawing at her innards, Tonya had begged Hatch to spare her life in exchange for merging into one being. Their pact, forged by magical energies concentrated by the Staff of Storms, created the first human-dragon hybrid.

A good thing too. Without me, you'd be no fun. C'mon, let's fly!

She clamped her chattering teeth. *Never.*

All summer and fall, she'd resisted Hatch but felt all his urges. Once, his lust for raw meat overcame her, and she'd gorged on uncooked beef. Since then, she ate vegetarian to annoy him, despite her meat cravings. She could resist but never escape these new dragon desires.

Gold and gems made her mouth water. Sometimes, she yearned to smash the jewelry store window, grab the treasure, and fly off. Oops. Walk off. Never fly.

Humans have yearned to soar since they climbed down from the trees.

Don't *lecture* me, little *Hatchling.*

I'm maturing supernaturally fast. Consider me a teen genius.

Genius? Tonya snorted.

If you're so smart, how come you let Marta Ashton bully you? You're twice her size, Hatch asked. *Why not hit her?*

That's not how it works with people.

Bullied child of an outcast mother, painful memories tangle your mind, Hatch whispered inside her head. *Let me erase them. You'll feel much better.*

Sensation returned to Tonya's legs, and she stumbled to the door. Locked.

Don't worry. I knew the door would lock behind us.

You did?

Calm down. Let me take control.

No.

I can get us down.

No.

Fine, but it could be days before somebody comes onto the roof, and I'm starving. Aren't you?

Low-grade hunger accompanied Tonya everywhere since she and Hatch had combined. At his suggestion, pangs ignited her abdomen. She had to eat now! Bloody steak, raw roast, ground hamburger. Her mouth watered, and her stomach roared for raw flesh.

That's my girl. We can pick up snacks on the fly. Ready to taste freedom?

No. Making me hungry is a dirty trick. She crossed her arms across a raging bellyache. If she suffered, he suffered too. The best strategy was to wait him out.

Twenty minutes later, she stamped her feet and clapped her hands to stave off frostbite. With most students asleep or in class, it could be many hours before anyone visited the forbidden roof. Cheeks stinging with the cold, Tonya glanced at the fire escape two stories below. Her head spun, and she backed away. The drop had to be twenty feet. If she jumped and didn't land perfectly, it would be her last argument with Hatch.

Don't be stupid. Surrender control and let me fly us down.

Something was very wrong when Hatch sounded like the voice of reason. She shuffled up to the edge, squinted at her tiny target, closed her eyes, and jumped.

2

Tonya missed the narrow metal staircase, but one leg caught on the railing, and she slid like a pair of scissors severing a sheet of paper. She gasped, flailing to grab hold, but momentum sent her tumbling again, her arms and legs clutching at air until one arm hooked a banister and she grabbed it.

She swung a leg over the top, her chilled hands prickling as the cold leached away their strength, and her fingers slipped.

Hatch snickered as, despite her best efforts, one hand let go.

No.

Then the other.

With a shriek, she fell, rolling as she landed on a pile of snow left by the plow.

When she raised her head, she spotted a wide-shouldered blonde in a tuque sailing over the snowy walkway on his long legs. Her boyfriend, Drake, reached her and leaned in so close, she sank into his blue eyes.

Why was he here?

Aching with bruises, she dusted powdered snow off her pajamas and forced a smile. "I meant to do that."

Drake thrust out his hands to offer a hug.

She didn't budge. "You were watching me?"

"I've been worried."

"Why didn't you help?" Blood rushed to Tonya's face. "You could have gone upstairs and opened the door to the roof!"

"You jumped from the *roof*?" His eyebrows raised, and he cupped her face between rough fingertips. "Were you trying to kill yourself?"

His blue eyes on hers felt too intense. She flinched away. "Of course not."

"Come with me to Health Services."

"I'm fine. Look, I'm not hurt." She flexed her arms.

"I'm not leaving until you talk to a doctor."

"I was goofing around on the roof, and I fell."

"In your pajamas?"

"It was stupid, okay, but you know me. Have I ever seemed depressed before?"

"No." He took off his coat and helped her into it.

"When my mother was in jail or when they took away my powers, did I ever think about taking my life?"

"No, but I don't believe this was an accident." He took her hands in his. "Tell me what's wrong."

"I'm fine." With a show of bending and stretching that sent pain through her legs, she proved her bones unbroken. "See?"

He traced her cheek with his thumb. "There are bags under your eyes."

That tender look had triggered a hundred kisses, but she had to stay strong and keep her distance. "Aren't you planning a movie with Zain?"

"I'd be with him if you answered my texts."

She yearned to apologize for worrying him. How good it would be to throw her arms around Drake and confess, but that would mean explaining Hatch. "I've been busy."

"That's it?" He raised his voice. "That's all you're telling me?"

"I don't need supervision."

Drake swallowed his retort and walked away, his breath visible in the chilly air.

Tonya blinked back tears and bit her lip as Hatch's laughter filled her head. "Wait!" She ran after Drake, pajamas flapping in the cold.

Halfway up the cement path, she reached him. "Sorry I didn't answer your texts." But she'd read them, staring at her phone in the middle of the night. "It's been crazy getting my assignments done before the holidays." A year ago, they'd have worked on them together, trading sweet whispers in the campus library.

His blue eyes lacked their usual sparkle, but his voice held steady. "I got a job at a camera store for the holiday rush."

"That's great."

"In Toronto. I came to say goodbye in person."

She went to hug him, but he stepped away. "I won't be back until the New Year."

The tension in her shoulders relaxed. "We can get together after the holidays."

He searched her face. "What's his name?"

Did he know about Hatch? "Who?"

"The secret boyfriend taking up your time, shutting off your phone, making you skip classes."

"Don't be silly."

"Check your activity. You haven't been posting. Priya never sees you outside of class, and two days ago, Zain saw you streak out of the woods at midnight, wrapped in a newspaper. If there's another guy, just tell me."

There had been unexplained snow on her boots that morning… Recently, she'd awoken on the pier staring at the full moon. Heart thudding, she checked her phone for activity in the evenings.

Nothing.

"I'm so sorry." Hatch had hijacked her body many times without her consent, leaving blanks in her memory. This was bad, very bad. "There's no secret boyfriend, but I have been dealing with a problem."

"Let me help."

"You can't."

"If you won't let me in… I gotta pack my bags."

There was no point following Drake again. Meanwhile, Hatch shouted demands in her head.

Give me your nights, or I'll lock you on the roof every morning.

Shut up, Hatch. She didn't have time for this. Drake talked like it was over.

Say yes, or I'll use your body against Drake, and Priya, and all your friends.

No.

You won't even remember hurting them. Hatch's raspy laughter echoed inside her skull. *Refuse all you like. I get stronger every day.*

Hatch was right. She couldn't hold him off forever.

Where had it all gone wrong?

3

Things had been much simpler on the first day of term. Rain slicked the red sandstone walls of University College, and water streamed down its leaded windows. The impressive rectangular building stretched between two towers. Gargoyles glared from the eves, their stone mouths gushing onto unwary pedestrians.

Tonya escaped the rain through an ornate archway and paused to close her umbrella. Hallways ran across the front and along two sides of the building, which sheltered a grassy courtyard. It had been raining all night. By now, the grass would be soaked and spilling water onto the stone floors of the covered arcades, so she stayed indoors. It was a good thing Professor Ferrier's plant lab was underground.

She chose the right-hand hallway, passing oak-paneled walls and a worn stone staircase. Mundane students crowded the musty corridor lined with lecture rooms on both sides. They chatted before their classes in economics and history, unaware of secret tunnels beneath their feet. The longest led west and under the river before it branched into catacombs under City Hall.

Eager for a fresh start, Tonya raced through the corridor, boots squeaking on the wet stone floor. In summer school, she'd relied on others to activate the hidden doorway leading to underground classrooms where Old Family students learned magic.

Never again. Breath held, she approached the trophy case at the end of the hall. Outside the building, the Staff of Storms drained away her powers, but Mayor Ashton had granted Tonya special permission to use her magic at school. She placed a trembling hand on the glass beside fingerprints left by previous students. *Would it work?*

Sensing her power, the trophy case shimmered and disappeared. An illusion charm bent the light so that as Tonya stepped forward into a hidden elevator, Mundane observers saw her disappear around the corner.

The wooden contraption creaked as it sank. Through a knothole, she watched herself descend through layers of stone and dirt until the temperature dropped. Fifty feet below the university, the doors opened, and a green scent beckoned Tonya along a chilly stone hallway.

Since Loon Lake had opened to outsiders, a gifted array of visiting lecturers clamored to live and work on top of its powerful conjunction of ley-lines and ancestor magic. The administration capitalized by instigating a visiting lecturer program, but one academic drew the most attention.

Students from first year to grad school balloted for spots in Professor Ferrier's once-in-a-lifetime class. Considered a genius, he was famous for discovering an Amazonian water plant that compounded life energy. He could shield and manipulate life forces but was famous for innovations in plant magic.

The floral notes permeating his lab promised Tonya a sweeter future. *Could he teach her to control her powers? Could he advise her on what to do about Hatch?*

Arriving early, she hoped to speak to the prof about her challenges controlling magic, but students filled four rows of lab benches facing the professor's marble-topped worktable. She was looking for a seat when Ferrier entered, a youngish prof wearing jeans and a rumpled jacket over a Flaming Lips shirt.

"Over here." Tonya's best friend, Priya, waved from behind a huge textbook. She had snagged the front bench in the center row—of course. Priya wouldn't be happy until she got the best mark in class—or at least a better mark than any of the guys.

"Can't we sit in the back?" Tonya asked.

Taking up extra space to store their bad attitudes, Marta and her Mod clique stared at Tonya from one side of the room. With them at her back, Tonya would spend class wondering what nasty tricks her longtime bully was planning.

Slender and athletic from training for the diving team, Marta turned heads with her full lips and long dark hair. Dressed in fashionably ripped jeans and a graphic tee, the mayor's daughter spent more monthly on casual clothes than most students paid in rent.

Priya finger-waved at Marta, shooting her a sarcastic grin. "Never mind them." She smiled at Tonya, her long black hair pulled into a ponytail that accentuated the symmetry of her light brown, heart-shaped face. For a lab class, Priya had traded her usual goth lace and Victorian skirts for a black dress shirt and slacks. Her trim figure would look elegant in anything.

Tonya had layered jeans and a pink hoodie over her tall hour-glass frame. She liked the way it hid her small waist and curvaceous figure, so creepy men didn't stare in the street. She also needed washable clothes. Ferrier's course description promised a hands-on experience where dirt flew, and arcane plants might grab the trowel and fight back. At least they wouldn't be bored, and Tonya was prepared to study. She flashed Priya the cover of Ferrier's latest book *The Real El Dorado: A History of Magical Plants in South America*.

"Teacher's Pet! I would never buy a prof's book in a pathetic attempt to make him like me." Priya unzipped her backpack, nonchalantly placing her own copy of *El Dorado* on the lab bench. "They say it's a real page-turner."

Ferrier introduced himself and, as he described his hands-on teaching philosophy and listed his office hours, warmth spread through Tonya's chest. He seemed nice and ideally skilled to tame her powers—assuming she could keep up with his advanced course. Priya would help.

Tonya glanced at her friend, and they shared a smile. Born in Toronto to Indian parents, Priya had begun as a Mundane, until time spent in Loon Lake awoke her talent for seeing ghosts. That wasn't all. When a handsome senior, Roberto, discovered her powers, he had courted her and became her boyfriend. Hiding outside the studio while Priya soldered her sculptures, Roberto had manipulated Priya's dreams and turned her into a conduit to transform matter using lightning.

Tonya would never forgive him for the way he betrayed her friend, but he had unleashed her powers. Sometimes it amazed Tonya that Priya never wanted revenge. Even after Roberto deceived her, Priya remained positive and focused on her feminist studies courses and sculpture projects.

Prof. Ferrier lectured without notes. "Living things are a prime source of magic, but we shouldn't drain life force indiscriminately." He glanced at Tonya, and suddenly the cavern chill felt colder. How much had they told him?

Everyone from the Old Families knew Tonya had extinguished a revenant with Helen, her birth mother, but they didn't know Tonya's out-of-control powers had killed a dragon. The guilt still haunted her. If Barbara, the aunt Tonya grew up calling "mother," hadn't forbidden it, magic training would have taught her to subdue the raging beast without killing.

Priya nudged Tonya's attention back to the professor, who set pots of daisies on each lab table.

"Today, we transform plants. Each of you manifests different capabilities, and those channeling life energy may find it a challenge underground. But trust me, it's safer." Again, his glance strayed to Tonya.

"Excuse me, professor, but why transform a flower?" Marta wrinkled her nose at her daisy.

Her lab partner, Arjun, sniffed the petals suspiciously. He had been a close friend of Priya's before joining the young Mods led by Marta. Since then, Tonya wasn't sure of his loyalties.

The professor gestured at a potted daisy. "You can transform it with charms, infuse it with life force, treat it with potions, make it bear fruit—anything your creativity suggests. This is a challenge, so impress me. It's worth 5% of your term mark."

"I've got this." Priya grabbed the daisies, and who could blame her? Priya had a grade point average to sustain, and Tonya was a magnet for magical catastrophes.

Half an hour later, Ferrier called individuals to his table to demonstrate. Arjun made his daisy turn blue, and Shin, captain of the diving team, made his mime the backstroke with its tiny stems.

The class applauded and Priya, who used to date him, wolf-whistled as he took a bow.

With the show over, Tonya gathered her books when Ferrier called, "Tonya, show us what you can do."

Nerves glued Tonya to her lab stool.

"Go on." Priya gave her a friendly nod.

Forcing her shoulders back, Tonya strode to the front of the room. *Never let them see you sweat.*

The plant felt very light on her palm as she probed it for life energy. A black space in her mind opened where inert things stayed black, and energies glowed in shades of green. The stone floor and walls lacked life, but the students pulsed neon green. Her greedy ability reached out, and hungry pathways snaked between her and her classmates like invisible roots, poised to drain their life force on contact.

Reeling and throwing out her arms, Tonya cut the connection, dropping the pot. She opened her eyes to see the daisies on the floor in a pile of dirt. "Sorry."

In a shocking display of maturity, Marta didn't comment.

"Pick up the plant." Ferrier watched closely, probably looking for signs she was losing control.

Tonya cradled the tender greenery in her hands, careful not to touch the roots. "What am I supposed to do?"

"Pop it in water so it doesn't dry out." He proffered a vase. "Let's see you draw power from something small."

"I can't." Her heart raced. What if she lost control?

"Sense the energy inside the plant." The professor made his hands hover around the vase, surrounding hers without touching.

This time, when she opened her mind, she only sensed the plant's life force, while Professor Ferrier blocked outside energies. With relief, Tonya concentrated on the faint glow of the dying daisy. Reaching out a magical tendril, she reduced it to dust and a puff of fog.

"Bravo!" Priya clapped.

"It's a start." The professor crossed his arms.

"Yeah, good job Tonya." Marta nudged a diving teammate. "Now you can get a job killing people's gardens."

4

Nothing Marta said could spoil the mood as Tonya and Priya walked west out of campus, past the cemetery and over the River Bridge, the boundary between Loon Lake's newest and oldest areas.

"Wait." Tonya stopped halfway across the bridge. "Look back."

"What am I supposed to see?" Priya shaded her eyes, facing office buildings in the distance.

"I like to savor the moment I leave." The Greater Loon Lake Area was a bustling city of 135,000 people, with most of that population living in custom houses, small subdivisions, or surrounding farms.

Hatch had forced her to fly over every acre with her heart hammering against the plates of her dragon chest. Through parted claws, she'd stolen glances at the flat gray tops of shopping centers, tall buildings, and condo towers clustered downtown. Reddish brick paved the expansive farmer's market on the north shore of the lake. Uptown and spreading in tidy grids to either side of downtown, shops, services, pubs, and restaurants attracted a busy tourist trade.

Beyond them sprawled streets dotted with houses, leafy backyards, and tiny blue swimming pools. In a ring beyond the single-family dwellings stood warehouses, townhouses, more condo buildings, and small industrial complexes on the outskirts between city and farmland.

To the west of the campus, big houses adorned the southern shore of the lake, opposite downtown. Past them, the land supported a mix of modern houses and historic homes, farmland, forests, and rivers and lakes carved by the receding glaciers.

"Do you feel it?" Tonya asked. Leaving the Mundane world of Loon Lake and entering magical Loon Lake Village always gave her a shiver.

"I don't feel anything," Priya admitted.

"You will once we get past the wall." Tonya led her friend over the bridge.

"Now I feel it." Priya winked. "The excitement of shopping! I have lots of nieces and nephews to buy for."

"I didn't think you celebrated Christmas."

"Not the religious part, obviously, but giving presents is creative. If I can make a gift, I do, but choosing the perfect thing for someone is also an art."

They wanted to explore the boutiques of the Old Town. Unfortunately, as they left the bridge behind and continued west, throngs of tourists and protesters clogged the streets between City Hall and the invisible barrier surrounding Loon Lake Village.

"It's like Blue Jays Way on a game night." Priya stopped a bearded man in Hawaiian shorts. "Where's the crowd coming from?"

"Everywhere." He hurried on.

The next person Tonya faced wore a polo shirt with a travel company logo. "Bumper crop on the phantom cruise ship?" she asked, but he hurried away.

"It's not ghost technology," Priya said. "I thought you knew that."

"I'm not a magic expert." Her parents had made sure of it. "However it works, the ghastly thing reappears with more tourists every day. The Old Families aren't happy."

"So all this," Priya indicated a line of protesters wearing sandwich boards, "is because they don't play well with others?"

"They hate Donna's wall. If my father came back into town ..."

"Which he won't."

"But if he did, he couldn't meet me in Loon Lake Village. If he got too close, he'd forget it ever existed."

"That's so stupid." Priya had been living on campus when Mayor Ashton raised a wall around Loon Lake Village and fortified it with amnesia spells against Mundanes. "Do you think the protests will do any good?"

"City Council is afraid of Donna." Tonya couldn't blame them. With the Staff of Storms, Donna could capture anyone's power and use it against them. "The Mod faction supports her."

"What about Mods with homes in Loon Lake Village?" Priya asked.

"What homes? For a hundred years the Trads outlawed their magic and kept the best jobs and properties for themselves. Before the Ashtons, Mods lived on the fringe, hiding their magic use."

"Then they should be kinder to the poor Mundanes who have lost everything."

"Agreed." Tonya had seen clips on the Old Family news app. Amnesiac Mundanes wandering the highway, homeless and lost until Ashton Security shuttled them to Toronto to clean up the streets. "I hate those bullies."

"A victim who gets power can turn into the worst bully." Priya pointed at Tonya, grinning. "That must be why you're such a jerk!"

Priya's sarcasm reminded Tonya of Zain, Drake's buddy. She'd drifted away from her friends since Hatch came into her life. "Wanna meet up with the Ninjas later?"

"Sure."

"Hey, hey, ho, ho, Mayor Ashton has got to go!" chorused a line of protestors. One man shouted into a megaphone, "Restore Mundane property! Reunite families!"

"No heavy sign to carry. That's clever." Priya pointed to a protest banner floating above them. "But I don't get the cartoon."

On the charmed fabric, a caricature of Mayor Donna morphed into a rhinoceros with an amethyst-tipped horn. Charging to life, it trampled Victorian houses and chased terrified Mundanes out of town.

"City Council declared that abandoned Mundane property would go to the next of magical kin. With a few well-connected exceptions, Mundane friends, roommates, and coworkers have been pushed out of Loon Lake."

"And you want *me* to shop here?" Priya halted. "My family is Mundane."

"You have magic now, and the National Council Rep overturned Donna's decree and restored my powers."

"Can we trust him?" Priya played with her braid. "He was creepy."

"To perfection. He scared Donna!" He'd also granted the Ninjas honorary Old Family status to recognize their assistance in cracking the murder case against Helen. Donna could no longer erase their memories or block their access.

Priya turned around. "We should boycott this place."

"I know you hate injustice, and I love the way you oppose oppression, but think of the shop owners. They didn't ask Mayor Ashton to do this. We should go after the mayor, not her victims."

Priya's face lit up. "We can still go to the magical toy store!"

Near the wall the crowds thinned, and Tonya noticed Mundanes get a confused look as they approached the charmed gate. It made her want to slap the mayor. In interviews, Mayor Ashton encouraged unhappy Loon Lakers to join their loved ones in the Mundane world, where their hatred of magic would make them "fit right in." She claimed her actions brought justice for the Mods who had suffocated under Trad rule.

"Restore magic for Loon Lakers!" she cried at rallies, conveniently forgetting the Mundane majority.

But it was stupid to let Donna's victory sour the mood, especially when Hatch could take everything away from her. In this moment, Tonya could enjoy peace. She was shopping with her bestie, and just being with Priya made her feel better. She was like the sister Tonya wished she had.

Even the Ashton guards smiled as they passed through the gate. Tonya finally had a professor who could help her control her powers, a boyfriend who loved her, and the Digital Ninjas were planning to make a new horror movie. No one, not even Mayor Ashton, could ruin this day.

They strolled the cobbled streets of Loon Lake Village, passing restored Victorian shops and cafes on either side. New scaffolding on the Village Inn drew Tonya's attention, until Priya took her arm and led her across the street.

"Look, a stationery store."

"*You* need paper?" Her friend took notes on a laptop.

"They have blank notecards for painting."

Inside the cozy shop, Priya compared card sizes while Tonya picked up a charmed eraser shaped like a cat. It trotted to the edge of her palm, poised to jump and meowed, but when she set it down, it turned back into an eraser.

"Have you seen these?" Tonya asked, but Priya had already reached the register, where a box of jeweled hair clips caught Tonya's eye.

"Ooo, sparklies!" It was Hatch's influence, but Tonya lifted each hair clip turning it this way and that to catch the light. She hated feeling this way, but she wanted them, needed them, couldn't put them down. Flushing, she dug her hands into the pile and let the sparklies flow through her fingertips like treasure.

"Are you going to buy those?" The clerk had finished with Priya, and Tonya was holding up the line.

"Sorry." Regretfully, she returned the bejeweled clips, crisis avoided, but when she emerged into the September sunshine, Priya dragged her into the worst store of all.

Like a rerun of Tonya's nightmares, they faced a display window loaded with diamond rings, necklaces, and earrings. All that silver. Gold. Platinum.

Tonya followed Priya into the jewelry store, licking her lips.

"What do you think?" Priya modeled a rhinestone tiara.

"Very shiny." In every direction, gold and gems called to her from elegant display cases. Heart thudding in her chest, Tonya had to leave before Hatch made her steal something. But if she fled, Priya would know something was wrong.

Another part of her, the accursed Hatch part of her, yearned to stay. It drew her from the display of gold earrings to a case bursting with diamond and ruby rings. From deep inside, the urge rose to smash the glass and flee with the treasure.

It would be so easy. Give me treasure.

Shut up, Hatch!

He refused to understand theft was wrong. His urges rose inside her. Torn between desire and panic, her breathing ratcheted up until her head spun. Seeing black, Tonya dropped her head between her knees and slowed her breaths to ease the panic attack.

"Are you okay?" Priya placed a warm hand on Tonya's back and held it there until she stood up.

"I'm fine." The attacks were coming more frequently, but slow breathing helped. Eyes unfocussed, she visualized something other than gold, rubies, and diamonds.

Smooth water.

Cute puppies.

Drake's eyes.

But the water sparkled like diamonds, the puppy's fur shone like gold, and Drake's loving eyes glistened sapphire blue. An open case of silver jewelry drew her over, with Priya trotting behind. Hatch hollered for treasure, and she wanted it as badly as he did.

"Do you have a tissue?"

While Priya fumbled in her purse, Tonya slipped a fat silver ring into her pocket.

Hatch had forced her to steal!

It wasn't too late. She could still put it back. The shopkeeper hadn't seen her. No harm done. Her brain sent the instruction to her hand to reach into her pocket, but it didn't move. Hatch blocked her in every way and confused her with the mounting desire to get home and guard the treasure.

Tonya rushed out the door, dry heaving. She staggered to a lamppost wreathed in disgusting gunk from last night's tourists, a rainbow slick of greasy spell remnants that pooled between the cobblestones and clung to her shoes.

"Are you drunk?"

"No!"

"It's just ... you're acting so weird lately." Priya held out her hand. "How can I help?"

Tonya wanted to let her, but Priya was too smart. If she said too much, her friend would guess Tonya's shameful secret. "I have a headache and need to lie down. Can I leave you to shop on your own?"

"Let's walk home together."

"Don't be silly." Priya was kinder than Tonya deserved. "It's not far to the dorm, and the walk will help clear my head."

"Let me give you a pain pill."

"It's fine. I have everything I need."

Everything but a trove of gold and gems to sparkle in the light, and Hatch wouldn't relent until she got one.

5

Tourists enjoying the fall colors thronged Loon Lake Village's traditionally quiet thoroughfares, forcing Tonya to dodge and step off the sidewalk. Leaving through the magical gate, she hurried through the noise and crowded gardens of City Hall, not pausing until she reached the bridge.

Facing east gave her a side view of the massive cruise ship that brought magic-using tourists to Loon Lake. Towering like a skyscraper, the vessel partially blocked her view of the public beach on the north shore. It floated like a fifteen-tiered wedding cake, decorated with a turquoise swimming pool and hot tub on the top deck.

How could the Mundanes miss it? She watched as a fishing boat trolled slowly toward the side of the ship and disappeared. Moments later, it reemerged on the far side unchanged, fishing lines still in the water. By what enormous arcane force could people enter an object of great power carrying hundreds of practitioners without noticing?

Hatch's dry chuckle interrupted her thoughts. *Curious monkey. Forget the boat and get me more treasure!*

The gold lust increased until Tonya couldn't stand it. She needed help, but Mundane doctors with their MRI scans and x-rays had failed to detect a problem. Until he started to shift, Hatch was a nagging voice in her mind without physical form. He couldn't be cut out like a tumor and, annoying as he was, Hatch had convinced her that he was special, beautiful even—when he wasn't forcing her to fly or threatening to harm her friends in dragon form.

Why do you have to be evil?! She aimed her thoughts at Hatch, but he only answered when it suited him. *Get out of me!*

All she wanted was her life back. Without Hatch she'd be free to date Drake safely, make movies with the Ninjas, and spend her weekends shopping with Priya and Grace. She even looked forward to eating her Helen's infamous cooking. But she could enjoy none of those things until Hatch stopped threatening to make her shift and harm her loved ones.

Until she found a way to remove Hatch without killing him, Tonya couldn't be free. In the meantime, she knew one person with the ability to charm animals. Maybe her birth mother, Helen, could get into Hatch's head and tone down the gold lust that was making her crazy.

Tonya hurried across campus, avoiding eye contact with anyone she knew. Heading west above the south shore of Loon Lake, the footpath ran through the cemetery, but she skirted around the iron gates continuing closer to the beach. Too many ghosts hated Tonya for burning down the Three Century Ash. On the east side of Kenny Road, near the bridge she and Priya had crossed earlier, Tonya strode across the fresh asphalt of a familiar parking lot.

Helen's Herbal Healing Shop used to be a log cabin with a long glass counter crammed with arcane novelties. The vinegar pong of jars crammed with flesh-colored forms used to fascinate Tonya, but Helen never told her what they contained.

A modern drugstore had replaced the cabin, but Helen still lived over the store, a glass-and-cement rectangle rising three stories against a backdrop of evergreens. A tone chimed as Tonya entered. Aisles of health food boxes and snacks in silver foil lined her path to the back counter.

She slipped around it and found the fire door unlocked. No witch of Helen's caliber feared thieves.

At the top of an iron staircase, a polished oak door opened into Helen's home. After the first store burned, she had rebuilt using an improbably generous insurance settlement. The way Helen influenced Mundanes sparked Tonya's disapproval, but she couldn't protest. The fire had been Tonya's fault.

A shiny new SCUBA tank and flippers hung from a peg beside a raincoat in the entranceway. In July, they should go diving together, assuming she and Hatch hadn't killed each other before then. With a shiver, she wrapped her arms around herself.

The living room featured refurbished antiques and flooring made of recovered barn board. It was a generous rectangular space with a high ceiling overlooked by bedrooms on the second story. An area rug, leather couch, and a cluster of chairs created a cozy nook facing the stone fireplace.

At the far end, Helen stood in a white kitchen, her figure long and lean compared to Tonya's tall hourglass. Leaving a pot on the stove, Helen greeted Tonya with a kiss on the cheek, her long white hair nearly identical to her daughter's. "How are you? Stay for dinner?"

"Sure," Tonya answered, before she noticed the burning smell.

"Can I get you a drink?"

It was weird sitting at the coffee table sharing a bottle of Chilean red with Helen—something she'd never do with Barbara. Since Tonya had discovered her powers, the woman she once called Mom now shunned her.

Before Tonya discovered her true parentage, Helen had acted like a hip aunt, introducing Tonya to minor charms and spells to practice when they could evade Barbara's supervision. Helen had given Tonya her first summer job, at the original Herbal Healing Shop, and taught her to sew charm sachets on an antique treadle sewing machine to preserve the magic.

The burning smell intensified, so Tonya checked the stove. Macaroni clung to the bottom of the pot, which had boiled dry.

"Sit down and enjoy your wine. I've got this." Helen gathered butter and milk to augment the cheese powder packet on the counter.

While she could influence animals and some humans, Helen's powers failed in the domestic sphere. Since her insurance windfall, a service cleaned her home. A dinner invitation meant drinks, snacks, and ordering in. It was the opposite of

Barbara, who saved every penny, but Helen was celebrating after years of hardship. Who could blame her?

Under Hatch's influence, Tonya always felt hungry. She shoveled down the rubbery mac and cheese.

"Would you like more?"

Yes!

Hatch would eat the tablecloth if you let him. "No, thanks." Tonya refused to let him make her gorge on pasta.

"Is *he* the reason you've been avoiding me?"

Of course Helen heard Hatch's telepathic voice. So much for easing into the topic. "He's getting stronger. I've had blackouts. Today, he forced me to steal a ring."

She described her breakdown in the jewelry store. Helen knew about the dragon's eggs—everyone in the Old Families had celebrated when Tonya intervened and saved a handful of tourists.

What Tonya had hidden from her birth mother was how quickly Hatch was growing. "Can you get him out of me?"

Helen took Tonya's hands across the table. "You made a deal with this Hatch under duress, correct?"

"It was that or die." Donna had captured her powers before Tonya could save herself.

A storm gathered on Helen's brow, and she leaped to her feet. "This is Donna's fault. She brought the Alvarez's and their dragons to Loon Lake, and she used your powers to speed his development." Helen topped her glass to the brim. "Somebody should mind wipe that woman!"

"Does that mean I'm stuck with Hatch?"

"With magic deals, there's often a loophole. More wine?"

Hatch bounced inside her. *Yes, yes, yes. I want to get drunk!*

No. Tonya needed her wits.

"Have you tried drawing out his life force?"

"You mean kill him?"

"Drawing a little life force at a time might slow him down." Helen came around the table and put a hand on Tonya's forehead. *Get out of my daughter!*

Your idiot spawn combined us by magical contract. We can't be separated.

If a magic bargain created you, there must be a way to break it, Helen replied evenly.

I'll kill her first.

Helen's mouth was a small straight line. *You'd kill yourself, and if not, I would.*

"Thanks." For once, her birth mom had stood up for her.

Helen told Tonya she worried too much. "There has to be a solution. Ask your university professors for help. Tell them a tourist from the cruise ship cursed you."

"Can't *you* do anything?" If Helen, who used telepathy and controlled animals, couldn't tame Hatch, who could?

"You made a deal, and your word is your bond. That kind of magic can't be broken." Her frown brightened. "Dessert?"

"No thanks." The family nicknamed Helen's pie crusts cement slabs. "I should go."

"Wait. Did you hear about Gramps McVitie?" Helen launched into a graphic description of her cure for a client's bunions using bone-nibbling parasites. The way she injected the charmed creatures with an oversized hypodermic needle turned Tonya's stomach, so she changed the subject.

"What do you think of the cruise ship?"

"I want to know why tourists can use them to visit Loon Lake, but Paloma Alvarez won't sell me a ticket to leave on one."

"I did kill her dragon's mate," Tonya said. "Sorry... did you say Paloma's behind the cruise ship? I thought the Ashtons ran them."

"When she repealed the anti-magic laws for the Village, Donna assumed the Ashtons and her Mod cronies would be in charge. But the minute the law changed, the Alvarez family bought a cruise ship, the hotel, and the buildings on either side of their Condor Bakery."

"I saw a crew working on the hotel today."

"City Council granted them a permit to add ten stories. The Alvarez's run the ships to bring in the tourists, and soon they'll be able to give them a place to stay, a pub to eat in, and they're adding a second floor to the bakery—where I doubt they'll be selling Mundane donuts."

"Have you been spying on them?"

"Through the eyes of every cat I can recruit. The Alvarez's may have fooled Mayor Ashton, and they can sell all the cruise tickets they like, but they're not putting me out of the charm business."

A high-pitched tone announced customers entering the store. "I'll be back."

Tonya followed Helen downstairs to where Grace smiled gently at her boyfriend, Zain. His wide eyes and stiff black hair reminded Tonya of a startled hedgehog.

When Zain saw Tonya coming, he crossed and uncrossed his arms, put his hands on his hips, and fluffed up his hair. Arms still unable to rest, he grabbed a foil pack and ripped it open. Around a mouthful of organic potato chips, he drawled, "Oh hey, Tonya. I'm surprised to see you here."

"Your acting is terrible." Grace grabbed a handful of chips.

"That's why you're my star." He smiled at her, his eyes lingering on her face.

Grace had brown skin with cute freckles, clear green eyes, dark brown braids with blonde tips, and an adorable face. Was it any wonder Zain, guerrilla director extraordinaire, featured her in his no-budget horror flicks? When she walked into a room, people turned to watch like magnets seeking iron.

"Are you coming to the meeting?" Grace asked.

With the stolen ring burning in her pocket and Hatch's appetites to distract her, Tonya had forgotten about the Digital Ninja's latest movie project. "Sorry. I'm too busy."

"Priya said you had some kind of attack." Zain stood still, watching her face.

"It was just a headache."

"Sure you won't come? We could use your ideas tonight." Grace's frown wasn't an act.

A lump rose in Tonya's throat. She didn't want her friends worrying about her, but if Helen couldn't break the contract, nobody could help her.

6

In September, Professor Farrier couldn't find a loophole in the magical agreement, and with each passing month, Hatch's power increased. In October, he learned to make her pass out for moments at a time. By December, he took control of her body at night, flying her gods knew where. On random nights, she awoke in snowy fields—or in bed beside a pile of gnawed animal bones. Hatch's hunting trips had exhausted and nauseated her, but nothing he did in the past scared her like this new threat to hurt Drake.

She wrapped her arms around herself and shouted telepathically, *This has to stop!*

Or what? I can make you black out, turn into a dragon, and eat Helen for a midnight snack. Hatch's laughter rang in her head, reverberating her deepest fears.

There was no way to shield her family or her friends. Tonya couldn't read his vile, reptilian thoughts, but Hatch heard everything she thought and sensed every feeling, including her closeness to Drake, Priya, and the other Digital Ninjas. To protect them, she would do anything—including staying away from them.

Between her classes and assignments, and the struggle to steal a few hours of sleep per night, September, October, and November raced by. Christmas was ten days away, but Tonya ignored her friends' invitations and texts. The worst moment was when Drake came by unannounced and witnessed her leap from the rooftop.

As Drake trudged away from the Mackenzie residence, his red-and-black Nikes leaving prints in the snow, Hatch had won. Every day he got stronger until there would be no holding him back.

That's right, pitiful human. You will be gone, and I'll be a dragon before Christmas!

7

A RUSH OF POWER woke Tonya, and she wriggled her fingers against something rough and wet. A tree root? Her naked body stretched out on a bed of frosty leaves, and when she sat up cold wind tossed her hair. Ice chips in gray water lapped at the nearby beach, but she sensed the power coming from the deep woods behind her.

After months of feeling dead inside, the life force of every plant and animal pulsed up her arms like they were living antennas.

That shouldn't be happening. The Staff of Storms was supposed to divert her powers—but when Tonya closed her eyes, a constellation of green lights throbbed in her mind's eye. It was life force that glowed from the trees and the hibernating animals underground.

Gratitude washed over Tonya, and she leaped to her feet. The mayor had forgiven everything and restored her full powers!

It was what she deserved for saving the town from Jack Waldock. Instead, she'd been accused of murder, jailed, and finally released no thanks to Mayor Donna Ashton.

So, what had changed?

Had Helen found a way to influence the wicked mayor? Or maybe Ashton had realized how much damage her old pal Jack Waldock could have inflicted.

No. Donna Ashton didn't mind hurting people if it kept her in charge.

But if the mayor hadn't purposely restored Tonya's powers, something must have damaged the Staff of Storms. Whatever. This moment was too good to waste overthinking or even worrying where her clothes went.

Like a woman dying of thirst, she siphoned power from every root, branch, mammal, and bird, filling herself with magical energy until the excess lifted her off the ground. With a pirouette, she let waves of excess energy radiate off her so she wouldn't explode with the pleasure and power. How she'd missed that vital connection!

You are pathetic.

The early morning breeze sent shivers across Tonya's bare skin, and she smelled rotten fish. Of course, Hatch was behind this, causing her to black out with no memory of the previous afternoon or night. What did Hatch make her do? Her euphoria vanished as swiftly as it had arrived.

Got you again, loser! Hatch's laughter filled her head.

Tonya cast around for something to cover her body, finding nothing but dead leaves and snow. What if somebody saw her?

You can't take my body hostage! she shouted at Hatch telepathically. *That wasn't the deal.*

What deal? I was starving when I came out of the egg. I'd have said anything to end the hunger pains, but I made a mistake. I should have eaten your body and left you to die.

Donna had used the Staff of Storms to drain Tonya's powers into the egg, then watched with glee as the hatchling dragon grew at ten times the normal speed. In moments, it had matured enough to chew on Tonya's guts.

Hatch still wanted her dead, except now they shared a damp naked body on the verge of hypothermia. She hoped that when the cold wind burned her skin and froze her fingers, he felt it too. If Tonya's teeth chattered any harder, it would chip the enamel.

Tonya hugged her goosebumps. *You could have at least brought me clothes!*

Why? Hatch countered. *It's not my fault humans are feeble.*

And subject to dying from the cold. Her fingers were turning blue, and she couldn't stop shivering. Tonya needed to get warm and fast. But before she could return to the dorm, she needed to cover herself. A moldy maple leaf wouldn't cut it. So far, this end of the public beach was deserted on a cold December morning, but an early dog walker could arrive at any moment. Time to get out of sight.

She retreated into the woods and tiptoed through a mix of fallen leaves and frost, arms stinging and feet numb, until she was behind the marina with the boat rental place.

With a backward look for witnesses, Tonya emerged from the woods, rock in hand, and broke a pane of glass in the door. Careful not to cut her wrist on the glass, she slipped an arm through and unlocked it from the inside. Her cheeks heated despite the cold. Hatch was turning her into a criminal.

The owner of the boat rental already hated her for losing his new Sea-Doo, but she'd settled the debt with money borrowed from her father. Dad had offered to forget about the money—but she'd paid him back in installments. The move to Toronto had cost her dad plenty after Barbara left him to live with her Pure faction friends. Besides, Tonya hated taking advantage of anybody. She refused to "steal" from her father, so what she was about to do turned her stomach.

Breathlessly, she pawed through a rack of bikinis and shorts, looking for something warm. She'd have to repay the owner anonymously—otherwise everyone would know she had stolen a neon pink shirt, gray shorts, and flip-flop sandals. In the face of Hatch's schemes, it was all she could do to hold on to her law-abiding, good person, non-criminal self.

Once dressed, Tonya returned to the beach where an oblong shape bobbed near shore like a log on the waves. That was new. It was red and black, and obviously not natural. Tonya shivered, drawn to the object but also repelled. Every instinct warned her to look away, because once she saw the details, there would be no denying the terrible fact.

A wave rolled the object onto the beach, which resolved into a short squat body with dainty bare feet. Bluish eyes stared blindly at Tonya who could never mistake that signature red suit or mane of black hair. The corpse was Mayor Ashton. Her neck was at an odd angle, and three deep gashes cut across her belly.

Tonya stooped to examine the mayor's porcelain complexion, but unfamiliar freckles and blemishes marred the surface. The unfamiliar details looked impossibly sharp; it was like seeing through a magnifying glass. Tonya blinked and glanced across the gray water at the island. The view seemed too clear as well, as if her eyes were binoculars. Had last night's transformation changed her vision?

Dragon vision.

And you wonder why I hate your puny human form, Hatch scoffed. *Humans! So deaf and blind.*

Tonya was too distracted by her newly heightened sense of smell to pay attention. Pine forest mingled with cedar and wild mint growing near the shore. Mold and a whiff of dead shellfish tainted the crisp smell of frigid water.

Tonya had seen embalmed corpses at funerals and expected a dead body to smell, but the lake had washed Donna Ashton clean. It wasn't until she kneeled beside the body, the scent reaching maximum strength nearest the mayor's wounds, that she detected the scent of lake water mingled with the musk of an apex predator—the unmistakable odor of dragon.

Last night, a dragon had killed Mayor Ashton.

Did you do this? she accused Hatch.

No answer. He didn't even laugh.

Please, please let me not be a murderer. Hatch might have done it in dragon form. The thought raised her bile. They shared a body. They could share guilt. Had Hatch taken the hatred Tonya felt for Donna Ashton and used it to make her commit murder?

Tonya wanted to believe that Hatch, although disgusting and prone to hunting small mammals, would not murder a human in cold blood. Especially not Donna Ashton who had saved him with the Staff of Storms. So, a dragon had done it, but not Hatch.

There was only one other dragon in Loon Lake, and that was Hatch's mother. Flores lived on Grand Island, trained and controlled by Roberto Alvarez. A fearsome beast, Flores breathed fire and defended her cave, but Tonya doubted she had killed the mayor. Why would she? The Ashton and Alvarez families were allies.

It was Tonya who hated Donna. Had Hatch disconnected her inhibitions and let Tonya claw the mayor to death?

Sour fluid mounted in her throat, and Tonya chucked up in the bushes, eyes bright with tears. Donna was dead, and no matter how evil she was, she hadn't deserved mauling.

On heavy legs, Tonya returned to the beach to survey the scene. *Hatch, what've you done! Hatch?*

He didn't stir.

Hatch!

When she wanted solitude, he ranted and railed, but when she needed answers, he went silent.

The faint crackle of gravel announced someone approaching, so Tonya dashed back into the trees, flip-flops slapping with every stride.

Hatch might have murdered Donna, which meant Tonya was guilty of not controlling her body. Or maybe somebody else had killed the mayor. Either way, the tough fight she'd had to prove Helen didn't murder Jack Waldock had taught Tonya a hard lesson. In Loon Lake, nobody related to Helen would get a fair trial. As her child, Tonya was an outsider, no matter what she did. Trads hated her for using magic, and Mods hated her for coming from an anti-magic Pure family.

When local authorities discovered that a dragon killed Mayor Ashton, the perpetually warring factions would agree on something at last—Tonya's family was guilty. Either Helen made a dragon kill the mayor with her mind control, or Tonya did it in dragon form. Somebody on campus must have witnessed Tonya's transformations by now.

Before things went any further, Tonya had to know whether to turn herself in or fight for her freedom. It would be nice to ask the Digital Ninjas for evidence. They had recently hacked into the campus surveillance cameras to source "found footage" for their movie projects. But involving her friends might cause Hatch or City Council to punish them.

Tonya had to go it alone and evade capture until she could uncover the murderer.

8

On the map, the Loon River expanded into a more or less round lake with Loon Lake City on its north shore. Founded by tree-clearing, sawmill-running Irish settlers in the 1800s, it had always hidden magical secrets from the Mundane world. A different kind of European settlers, the Old Families, brought the bones of their ancestors with them across the Atlantic. Practitioners since time immemorial, these witch families kept to themselves in tiny Loon Lake Village, burying their dead in a grove of protective ash trees and preventing outsiders from getting too close.

That was a lot easier before Loon Lake City grew to a population of 135,000 fanning out from the north side of the lake. Downtown was fairly small, surrounded by suburban residences, mixed industrial areas, and beyond them, hobby farms, working farms, and forests.

It was the downtown portion of Loon Lake City that preoccupied Tonya on the frosty hike from the west end of the public beach back to campus. Bushy evergreens obscured much of her route west, but she hid her face on Kenny Road and rushed by the Herbal Healing Shop hoping Helen wouldn't spot her out of the top-floor window before she could cross the bridge.

When she felt the shoveled walkway under her flip-flops, Tonya took her first relaxed breath. With so many students gone home for the holidays, few would be up early enough to watch her dash by in shorts. If they did, the student habit of wearing shorts and flip-flops inside the dorms would disguise her walk of shame in stolen clothes.

Back in her room, dressed and wrapped in a musty wool blanket, Tonya went over the morning's events. Shouldn't there be blood on her hands if she'd clawed someone to death?

No. When Hatch's claws and scales transmuted back into human flesh, her skin never retained any dirt Hatch picked up hunting—unless he ate something nasty. For some disgusting reason, whatever was inside his body survived the change. The outside was different.

When Hatch forced her body to metamorphose, it ripped whatever clothing she was wearing, which dropped off in shreds. But to know whether Hatch murdered the mayor, she needed physical clues. Would traces of Donna's blood remain under Hatch's claws?

Hatch, change back into a dragon!

No response. To the one request he begged for. He didn't snicker or make sarcastic comments either.

Are you asleep?

Still no answer.

His silence was suspicious. Maybe she could trigger the change without his help. She knew the sensations that preceded transformation from fighting it off, and she'd undergone full transformation in her dreams when Hatch rode her at night.

First, a sweeping wave of pain paralyzed her limbs. Next, her bones broke, migrating and growing under her skin in a symphony of agony.

She tried to recreate that moment when change began, but nothing happened. And no wonder. Considering the pain it inflicted, transforming opposed every instinct for self-preservation.

Self-preservation. That was it. Tonya opened her eyes. *If Hatch refused to cooperate, she'd make instinct work for her.*

Sitting on the railing of the fire escape, Tonya peeped at the snow pile two stories below. If this failed, it would break her legs. She let her feet dangle in the chilly air, like a swimmer getting used to the water. All it would take was one little push …

Foolish human. I will let you plummet to the ground, and I'll laugh when your legs snap. You can't trick me.

Please, Hatch. I have to know whether we killed Mayor Ashton.

Don't ask questions if you can't handle the answer.

Teach me to transform.

Stick to killing plants, loser. Hatch's raspy chuckle made her scalp itch on the inside.

What did you make me do?

No, little ape. You haven't earned the right to ask me questions. We had a deal, and you reneged.

You failed to mention blackouts and murder when I spared your life.

I spared yours, and you promised to share this body. You chose day, and I chose night.

Not if you make me hurt people from sunset to sunrise.

Dragons live for hundreds of years, and you're getting weaker as I grow. How do you plan to stop me?

I can jump off this railing.

You wouldn't dare.

He was right. *I'll sleep in a cage every night, so you can't fly anywhere or kill anyone.*

Calm yourself. Too much hot temper and you'll start breathing fire.

You're bluffing.

Stupid human. Why can't you understand this power is a gift? Let me lead. I'll shift us into my proper, godlike form. Relax and relinquish control. The rest of your life can be beautiful and simple.

With you in charge, what happens to me, my family, my friends?

You won't need them when you become all dragon.

That wasn't what she wanted, and until she knew the truth, she couldn't trust anything he said. *Teach me how to change now!*

Give me control, and I'll transform us forever.

No. She'd never do that.

Then I won't teach you how to change.

Bad choice. Tonya stood on the railing and launched herself at the sky.

9

It takes under a second to fall two stories. Feet first and body relaxed to reduce the chance of injury, Tonya landed in a cascade of crunches and popping sounds as the bones in her legs and pelvis splintered. It was an experience few could survive, but she wasn't quite human anymore.

By the time Tonya peered through slit eyes, paralyzed by the pain, the broken bones inside her crunched and snapped as they lengthened, shortened, and migrated to new locations. Her feet and legs crushed by the fall transformed into powerful scaly thighs and shins, ending in taloned claws. The pain in her legs faded and migrated to new body parts as flesh shifted and grew, expanding her chest behind armor-like scales that glinted rainbow silver.

Ripped clothes dropped onto the snow pile, evidence of her rapid growth. But where was the blood? Her leg bones had splintered and broken the skin, but even using her heightened dragon senses she couldn't see or smell any trace of her own blood. Every cell of her body had transmuted into dragon form without leaving a drop of human bodily fluids behind. That meant her clean hands at the scene of Donna's murder proved nothing.

Pulse pounding in a chest big as an oil barrel, she sniffed under her claws for traces of Donna's ripped clothing or blood.

Nothing.

Her claws were as clean as a newborn armadillo's. Nosing each digit released nothing but a faint odor of snow. All that pain for nothing.

Okay Hatch, change me back before someone sees us.

Silly human, I'm starving. Time to hunt!

Tonya's screams came out in roars as they galloped to speed and leaped into the sky.

10

From rare sightings the frequency grew until the cruise ship appeared every morning, invisible to Mundane eyes. In anticipation, alert members of the Old Families trained their gaze on a spot near the public pier where the white ship shimmered into being.

Which meant that on this particular Tuesday morning, nobody was watching the clearing by the woods south of the cemetery. When a red pavilion popped into existence, sheltered by a ring of trees, not even the ghosts noticed.

In Loon Lake and beyond, practitioners studied the limitations of magic. It could rearrange but not destroy matter, and every spell required energy. To teleport even a teaspoon over a short distance demanded lots of magical power. So, when a sky-scraping cruise ship kept appearing on a northern lake best known for bass fishing, it intrigued the Stranger.

Standing in the snow in front of the red pavilion, he cast a warming spell on his woolen greatcoat and buttoned it up to his tie. His charmed dress shoes would repel slush and ice on the long walk into town.

He emerged from the woods below the cemetery, recognizing landmarks from the map. The waters of Loon Lake formed a rough oval seven miles across. A tree-covered island stood in the middle featuring a granite dome. At work, they'd warned him locals stopped visiting the island's beach and cave system when a dragon settled there. Smart move.

To his right, Loon Lake University stood on the south side of the lake, silhouetted by the rising sun. The original building was vintage sandstone with gargoyles on the eves and scores of leaded windows. Modern cement structures punctuated the south shore like scattered shoeboxes, but Victorian streetlamps lit the footpath along the lake. If he weren't here on business, it would be a nice place to go for a run.

Across the lake, downtown lights loaned their glow to a modest city clueless that the Old Families held it in an invisible web. Few buildings rose above ten stories, and residents mostly inhabited suburban enclaves or the farmland beyond. Where the lake narrowed, he could see a public beach, deserted except for the fifteen-story cruise ship glowing on the gray waves. It was an oddity so far from the ocean but probably not relevant.

Today, he would start with Loon Lake Village. Kenny Road ran north-south dividing old from new. It crossed River Bridge over the Loon River. Farther west, the water widened into a lake, making room for a public beach, a marina, the Ashton's private boathouse, and the Mod Clubhouse, all on the south side of the water.

Farther west and south of the beach, City Hall stood surrounded by a beautiful garden that enclosed a fancy greenhouse but also a jail. With maps and local lore to guide him, he knew that south of the invisible barrier surrounding Loon Lake Village the Ashton family compound stood inside its own wall.

He was tempted to buy breakfast at the farmer's market on the north side of the lake, but there was too much to do. It was nearly 8:00 a.m. as he watched a flotilla of revelers leave the cruise ship in motor launches. As they headed for the beach, one witch shot enchanted fireworks into the air, flouting local regulations. All the passengers in one boat sported Mardi Gras beads and brandished beer cups, turning their short trip into a floating keg party.

Ski-Doos shot out of the side of the ship, the personal watercraft enchanted to keep the riders dry. Several witches rode broomsticks off the top deck or simply floated in the air.

Pummeled by boats and spells, the ice surrounding the pier broke into chunks and floated away. Another boat reached the pier and released a choir of Christmas carolers wearing Santa hats. They sang their way off the dock and headed west for the bridge to take them into Loon Lake Village. Clusters of visiting practitioners streamed after them dressed in everything from sandals to snow pants.

The Stranger joined the flow of tourists as it filtered past City Hall and mobbed the entrance to Loon Lake Village, made up of twin gates visible only to practitioners. A trio of security guards tried to keep up with the flow but, overwhelmed, they waved everyone through.

As they emerged from the bottleneck, tourists in tie-dyed shorts and tees, charmed to repel the December chill, smiled and chatted, happy to be moving. On a nearby side street, pinned against the wall of a stately Victorian home by the crush of bodies, a witch in traditional black robes powered up a fireball. Before she could hurl it, the Stranger raised a hand. Eyebrows raised in alarm, she aborted the spell and melted into the mob.

The current of bodies flowing into Loon Lake Village prevented anyone from leaving. Shoppers packed boutiques. Lines at cafes and restaurants snaked out the doors. Venders at food stands and ice cream carts sold out and struggled to leave.

At a bar cart, a staggering witch slurred her request for a shot of espresso.

The well-dressed vendor spread his hands on the counter. "Sorry, dear. All sold out."

"Don't you 'sorry dear' me!" she screeched. "I'll turn your slick shoes back into alligators." Magic gathered around the witch's hands, sparking and setting fire to a nearby cedar hedge. The greenery combusted, kicking sparks in every direction.

With a raised hand, the Stranger quelled the fire.

The witch paled in a gratifying manner, but he had bigger fish to fry. He cautioned her and teleported her to the office. Few re-offended after meeting his coworkers.

11

Afternoon light streamed through Tonya's north-facing dorm window and roused her from confusing dreams—but reality was more disturbing. Twigs wet with saliva dirtied her pillow, and her stomach groaned and strained under pressure until she released a thunderous burp.

Weird, but not as strange as the aftertaste. Gamey and greasy with a soupçon of... hair?

Between her teeth!

Hatch!

He ignored her telepathic shout.

Answer me you creep! What did you make me eat?

Hatch remained silent.

After changing the sheets, she went to the communal showers to scrub her body clean. By the time she finished brushing her teeth with toothpaste and baking soda to banish the taste, it was nearly noon. Tonya opened the Old Family News App on her phone expecting reports of fighting in the streets. The murder of Loon Lake's most controversial mayor would drive an even bigger wedge between Loon Lake's opposing factions.

The anti-magic Trads and extremist Pures would blame the Mods, citing their reputation for black market deals and shady magic practices. Meanwhile, the

Mods had little motive to kill the woman who had returned magic to Loon Lake after the Trads had outlawed it for a century.

An objective observer might suspect the Trads or the Pures of murder, if they weren't such goodie goodies. They hated the mayor's policies, but Tonya couldn't imagine the Pure ladies of her estranged mother's coffee klatch ordering a hit on Mayor Donna Ashton.

But that wasn't why she couldn't look away from the screen, barely blinking for fear of missing something. The meat in the pit of her stomach made her queasy and reminded her how easily Hatch could make her blackout and do things she didn't remember. Waking for the second time this morning, Tonya didn't need coffee to feel wired. The phone shook in her hand, and her mind raced.

Had someone witnessed her leaving the beach? Her heart's desire—breaking free of Loon Lake—would never happen if she'd committed murder. Tonya went to the cupboard, grabbed a stale Kaiser bun, and chewed on the hard crust with her eyes on the phone as she sat at the splintery student desk that came with her room.

Tonya waited, but there were no accusations, no speculation. Instead, they ran a highlight reel of Mayor Ashton winning the election, her first day in office, and the ribbon ceremony for the charmed wall around Loon Lake Village. When they ran out of photo ops, they explored Mayor Ashton's humble beginnings, the establishment of Ashton Security, the building of the private magic-suppressing jail, and finished with a triumphant visit to the Ashton mansion when it was first built. The sight of Marta, the mayor's daughter, scowling furiously and slamming her door on the camera, made Tonya giggle. Served her right to show the world her bad temper on screen. Marta had bullied Tonya all through high school.

On and on the media portrayed Mayor Ashton's life story in smiles, parties, handshaking, and baby kissing. Instead of a ruthless narcissist who had dispossessed the Mundanes of Loon Lake Village, they depicted Donna Ashton as a poor girl made good.

Tonya expected the syrupy tributes, but why no statement from law enforcement? A murder, right after Loon Lake opened to outsiders, should have triggered an investigation by National Council. An outsider could have done this or a tourist.

But why? Plenty of Loon Lakers had reasons to bump off the mayor. It wouldn't take an outsider—but one of them might have seen something.

Blood rushed to her cheeks. From their cabin windows, anyone on the cruise ship might have seen her naked on the beach or watched her break into the boat rental.

Wait. No. The boat always disappeared in the middle of the night. It might not have returned by dawn. Groggy, her stomach aching, she went over her memories from earlier that morning. Had the ship been there?

It had.

Which was really weird when she thought about it. Why would the vessel stay overnight, for the first time, the same night Mayor Ashton was murdered? Coincidence or means of escape for a hired assassin?

Then there were the Mundanes. Ashton Security would be called in to manage the local police and erase the memories of Mundane witnesses. She had to find them and talk to them before Ashton Security!

Tonya threw on jeans and grabbed a pink tee out of her closet. If a witness had seen the guilty dragon, their description would prove whether it was Hatch. She stuffed her feet into thick socks and then boots before putting on her winter jacket. If Hatch had done this, Tonya would have to accept her portion of the guilt—but not until she was sure it wasn't Hatch's mother, Flores. She lived on the island—supposedly tamed since the summer when she kidnapped a handful of victims—but Tonya doubted it.

She glanced at the news app before leaving, but National Council still hadn't commented. Loon Lake City should be in turmoil until they caught the perpetrator, but the news anchor assured them in a deep voice there would be no investigation. The OPP and local magical authorities agreed. In a tragic incident, a rogue bear had mauled Donna Ashton to death.

A what?

Somebody knocked at the door, and Tonya knew they'd come for her. Fake news on the app was a smokescreen to put folks at ease and give National the advantage of surprise. With her longtime grudge against Mayor Ashton for jailing her and her mother, Tonya had to be their prime suspect.

She raked a hand through her long white hair and forced a smile.

12

TONYA LOOKED THROUGH THE peephole of her bare-bones dorm room. It wasn't an Ashton Security guard or an investigator from National Council—it was much worse. Right when Tonya needed to get out and discover the truth, the Digital Ninjas were knocking.

She searched the room for traces of Hatch's disgusting meal and cracked the window open before answering the door.

"Hi Tonya." Drake smiled shyly but didn't try for a hug. "Let us in?"

Tonya stepped back, and Priya breezed past her and sat on the bed. "I like the pink wall. When did you paint it?"

"A few weeks ago."

In a pathetic attempt to cheer yourself up, Hatch sniped.

The paint was for her, but she'd chosen Gustav Klimt posters enhanced with golden flecks and rings to appease Hatch's treasure lust.

At the desk, Zain took the spindly chair and balanced it on a back leg. Leaning against the splintered desk beside him, Grace glanced at Zain's antics, a smile twitching at the corner of her mouth.

"Grace, I love your hair." Her friend had traded in her braids and pony beads for a relaxed hairstyle that smoothed her medium brown hair and brought it past her shoulders. Tonya envied the limber way she moved, with strength that came from Pilates and training for fight choreography.

"Thanks."

Tonya faced Drake who, annoyingly, looked hunky and adorable at the same time. "I thought you were working in Toronto."

"I took a day."

"This is an emergency." Zain stood, thin and wiry, the tips of his hedgehog hairstyle making him almost as tall as Drake.

The intensity of all eyes on her was too much for Tonya. "Let's get out of here. We should go for a walk."

Nobody moved. So much for distracting them.

"We've been worried." Priya patted the bed beside her until Tonya sat.

Had they heard about the mayor? Tonya needed to get rid of her friends before the authorities arrested her and her buddies got dragged in as negative character witnesses. They knew Mayor Ashton had ruined her life and tried to get Helen executed.

Part of her, a deep subconscious part, might have wanted the woman dead. Could Hatch have used that dark side to make her kill the mayor? She hoped not. When she looked at Drake's sweet blue eyes and innocent face, she knew the right thing was to kick them out of her room and protect them from the coming storm. This wasn't their fault or their business, but if they hung around her too long, City Council would suspect them of something. They saw any friend of Tonya's as tainted.

Helen's bogus arrest and trial for killing Jack Waldock had proved it. The Old Families would never give Helen or her daughter a fair chance. Ashton Security would love to pin the mayor's death on Tonya or Helen to settle old scores.

Her inner turmoil had distracted her, and she realized Priya was talking. "I'm sorry. What were you saying?"

Priya tossed her shiny black pigtails. "That's not funny. We've been worried about you."

"We've invited you out, tried to involve you in our projects," Grace scoffed. "Do you think you're too good for us?"

"It's drugs, isn't it?" Zain rested his hands on Tonya's shoulders and peered at her face. "Her eyes are bloodshot. I told you!" he announced, a note of victory in his voice.

"You don't think I'm on drugs," she asked Drake, "do you?"

He sat on the other side of Tonya and took her hand. "Are you depressed?"

When she didn't answer right away, he apologized, moving in for a hug. "I never should have left you alone."

"Don't be silly." She pushed him back gently and stood. "I'm fine." She looked at the Ninjas. "You're overreacting. I've just been busy."

"It's the winter holidays," said Grace. "No exams or essays."

"Busy getting ready for Christmas."

Priya blinked. "Twenty-four hours a day?"

She wasn't cruel enough to say it, but she knew. Barbara was shunning Tonya, Dad had moved to Toronto, and there were no plans for a Christmas reunion.

"I need to buy Dad a gift."

"So, one gift, and Helen doesn't do Christmas."

"I'm getting her something anyway."

"You're too busy shopping to see us, but you haven't bought anything yet?" Grace's logic countered Zain's excitable nature, a perfect match.

Seeing them together made Tonya yearn to kiss Drake and make up, but that afternoon, with Hatch's disgusting bush meat still digesting in her stomach, Tonya doubted that was wise. To protect Drake, she had to break up with him. Hatch wasn't bluffing. If she didn't push her friends away, she would wake up one morning with metaphorical blood on her hands and not remember hurting them.

"Get out," she mumbled, gaining confidence as her certainty grew. "It's time for you to leave."

Drake's hurt look gutted her.

Zain spluttered at Tonya, "Are you crazy?" He glanced nervously at Drake. "You need us, and you need rehab."

"I'm not on drugs." She stood tall, striving to look offended. "And I don't need help."

Grace's jaw dropped. "C'mon Zain." She took his elbow and led him out, followed by Priya.

Drake didn't move, searching Tonya's face for something she could no longer give him. Pressure mounted in her chest, and she took a long, slow breath to tamp down the panic. Who would she be without him? What would she be if her love got him killed?

"You too, Drake. Get out!"

She slammed the door before he could see her cry.

13

Ordinary corpses can chill at a funeral home or the morgue for weeks without posing a threat to the living. This gives the family time to plan the funeral, contact mourners, and bring in relatives from out of town.

Old Families enjoyed no such luxury of time. To prevent confused ghosts from rising or other supernatural mishaps, they consigned their dead to the ground as swiftly as possible. Standard precautions made the arrangements simple. Members of the Old Families buried their dead in the family plots located in the oldest section of Loon Lake Cemetery. Until Tonya burned it down, the Three-Century-Ash had spread its branches over the plots like a leafy guardian, drawing the lingering life force out of the departed and filtering magical energies safely back into nature. Since losing the Ash's protection, magical families entombed their loved ones even more quickly, surrounding them with young ash trees, to avoid attracting dark entities hungry for power.

Wednesday morning, facing a crowd of Mundanes and Old Family members paying their respects, the Ashton brothers held a graveside service the morning after Donna Ashton's body was found. Shivering beside Helen, Tonya hunkered into her coat waiting for the eulogy to start. Hundreds had shown up to stand in the cold, although the crowd of bodies did little to stop the wind cutting through the long wool coat she wore out of respect.

The Ashton brothers clustered behind a podium with a microphone, facing the crowd. Their niece, Marta, stood off to the side. Red rimmed her eyes, and she'd pulled her dark hair into a ponytail. It was the first time outside of a swimming pool that Tonya had seen her without lipstick.

Can you believe Stephen? Helen crowed telepathically. *He's wearing gold chains and a warm-up suit at his sister's funeral!*

Why do you care? It was in bad taste to mock the mourners, even if nobody else could hear them.

Helen elbowed Tonya. *With all that money, doesn't he own a suit?*

It's not our business. Marvin tiptoed around his younger sibling's short temper, accepting his vanity and the delusion that designer tracksuits could replace formal wear.

As the minister addressed the crowd, energy rippled through Tonya, raising the hair on the back of her neck. Since her powers had returned, every living thing pressed at her with a green, glowing life force, but this was a darker energy pulsing and red. She turned to find the source.

At the back of the crowd, a man with windswept hair wore a gray wool great-coat with twin rows of brass buttons down the front. He stood apart from the surrounding families.

Tonya caught Helen's eye and unfurled her fingers in the stranger's direction. "Do you recognize him?"

No. Maybe Donna had a thing for handsome weightlifters. Helen licked her lips. *Tasty.*

I hadn't noticed.

Ha! Pick up your jaw 'cause you just dropped it.

"Stop laughing and listen to the minister," Tonya whispered. "Uh oh. Now that guy is staring at us."

"We *are* stunning platinum blondes." Helen did a slow turn and winked at the man. "Let 'em stare."

Times like these made Tonya pine for Barbara. The mother who raised her wouldn't flirt at a funeral. Tonya scanned the crowd, looking for Mom's wavy brown hair, but couldn't spot her among the hundreds in attendance.

Whether they loved or hated the late mayor, every member of the Old Families had to pay their respects. Tradition had kept them together since they had sailed from Europe in the 1800s.

Among the mourners, Tonya recognized former Mayor Thornton wearing his iconic gray tie. Thornton should hate the Ashtons. Donna Ashton had made Stephen put him into a magically-induced coma, so she could take charge of the mayor's office. Any other man would have skipped the funeral or spit on her grave, but Tonya admired Thornton's toughness, calmly shaking hands and chatting with his former constituents as if they were all that mattered.

The Trad and Pure factions held grudges going back a generation against the Ashtons for supporting the thuggish necromancer, Jack Waldock. His death magic had turned Helen and Tonya's hair necro-white. He collected protection money and fireballed opponents, raising a tide of revenue that also buoyed Ashton Security's fortunes as they pretended to work against him.

Plenty of locals might have wanted to avenge themselves against the Ashtons for supporting Waldock in the bad old days—but if a Loon Laker did it, why hadn't Tonya seen or smelled evidence of human interference on the body? A dragon had wounded Donna—and few Loon Lakers could control such a beast.

When the minister invited the family to speak, Marvin strode to the podium wearing a designer suit, his dress shoes gleaming against the snow. He pulled his phone from the breast pocket of a long coat and spoke clearly, while Stephen stooped over his shoulder like a weepy buzzard.

"Donna was fifty-nine, but it feels like only last week we were teenagers, teasing our little sis for being short."

Stephen interrupted, "We said we couldn't hear her, because she was so close to the ground."

Marvin looked away, then back at his speech. "I regret not telling Donna how proud she made me." He cleared his throat. "We grew up near the dump in a house built from scrap. Clothes came from the Salvation Army or Walmart at Christmas. I didn't care, but it bothered Donna."

Behind him, Stephen nodded vigorously. "She had style."

A woman in the crowd shouted, "That hair!"

People laughed until Stephen stared them into silence. Dark circles underscored his bloodshot eyes.

Marvin scrolled to the next part of his speech. "In school, the magic teachers tried, but Donna had no powers."

Behind Marvin, Stephen muttered something.

"But she held her own." Marvin's voice went thin and reedy. "Kids used to follow her to the dump and call her Oscar the Grouch and Garbage Girl."

Stephen interrupted. "Now we have a family compound and a boathouse. Grandad started Ashton Security, but Donna expanded it."

"You tell them." Marvin ceded the stage.

After blowing his nose thoroughly, Stephen gripped the podium with both hands. An octave too low, he whispered into the mic. For a long moment, he stared, speechless, at the cemetery grass.

Is he shaking?

Tonya ignored Helen.

He's slurring his words.

"Donna was, uh ..." Stephen wiped his brow. "A great little sis. I hated her tourist policies, but she might've become a great mayor someday. I get that now." Stephen covered his face and stumbled away.

The minister cleared his throat. "Would anyone else like to speak before we return our dear sister Donna to the earth?"

"Marta?" Stephen looked at his niece, but she shook her head.

Since when is Marta at a loss for words? Helen sniped.

It was understandable after such a blow. Tonya's mother lived on, but their estrangement stung. Tonya had grown up calling Barbara Jones "Mom," never guessing she was Helen's.

The truth came out during the fight against Jack Waldock, and the three of them reunited, until Barbara ran away with the Pure faction and declared Tonya dead to her.

Tonya's grief couldn't equal what Marta was going through, but she empathized. The more she thought about the mayor's death, the harder it was to reason out who could have done it. She looked at the Pures, dressed in dull-colors and modest hemlines. They opposed fun of all kinds, especially magic.

As the incoming mayor, Donna Ashton had erased a century of policy when she legalized magic use in Loon Lake Village. The wall and amnesia spells to repel Mundanes angered folks with non-magical family members, but some Trads applauded. Before Donna, they learned magic only to defend the town in case of attack from the outside world. It was a skill they could never use, and an advantage they could never press. Mod bootleggers had always sold so-called herbal remedies, but now Trads could also brew and sell potions.

Barbara and the Pures didn't benefit. They believed any magic use attracted evil. When Tonya burned down the Three-Century Ash in her fight against Jack Waldock, they declared it a sign. Unless Mods and Trads renounced their spell-casting ways, magic would reassert nature's balance by attracting demons to punish them.

Barbara was wrong to agree with the fanatical biddies she lived with, but losing her mother hurt. The pain returned whenever a passing stranger reminded Tonya of Barbara. Like that frumpy woman with pale cheeks. When she turned, a side view of her face startled Tonya. It *was* Barbara with her hair cut short. Had she stopped plucking her eyebrows? Without lipstick, her mother's lips made a grim line.

Barbara noticed Tonya watching and turned away to face her clique of Pures.

After Marvin, political supporters and rivals made the expected speeches, but the mayor had attracted few real friends. Using broad nylon straps, pallbearers lowered the coffin into an irregular hole dug by hand. Nothing but the best for a rich Old Family funeral.

To conclude, Marvin, Stephen, and Marta each dropped a long-stemmed rose onto the coffin. The minister intoned a solemn prayer, and the groundskeeper dropped a shovelful of earth into the hole.

Afterward, people clustered in conversational groups or headed for cars parked beside the chapel at the top of the hill or along the roads. With so many in attendance, it would take time to clear out the vehicles.

Helen stared after the Ashtons, ignoring Tonya, who tried to take her arm and steer her toward the cemetery gate.

The father should have come home for his daughter's funeral.

"Did you know him?" Tonya had never heard Marta mention a grandfather.

He used to be charming. Helen's eyes sparkled. *He'd stagger into town after brewing illegal magic for days, and he cast outrageous spells on the island. Shocked the old folks like a proper rebel.*

No wonder Helen liked him. Maybe growing up with Aunt Barbara hadn't been so bad. She was judgy, but Mom never laughed at people's misfortunes.

Leaving Helen to gloat, Tonya cruised through the crowd, using her dragon hearing to learn what she could. If the murderer started bragging, Tonya needed to know, so she shadowed the Alvarez Family. Roberto Alvarez was the rich brat who had manipulated Priya for her magic. Paloma, the matriarch, had drugged Tonya with mind-enchanting pastries. Her slight husband, Victor, shrank behind his wife but never opposed her. They were nasty, power-hungry people who competed with the Ashtons for control of Loon Lake, but were they murderers?

Paloma and Donna had clashed over opening Loon Lake to foreign practition-ers of magic, because Donna built the wall to reserve Loon Lake Village for the Old Families.

The Ashton Clan thought they were collaborating with the Alvarez family. They had allowed Paloma and Roberto Alvarez to secretly raise a pair of "fire salamanders" on the island, not knowing that Roberto could manipulate Priya's magic and transform them into mature dragons. Flores, trained by Roberto to do air patrol, broke the Ashton's monopoly on local security and forced them to compromise. For a while, Ashton Security kept the jail cells under City Hall running by using the Staff of Storms to capture and diffuse criminals' powers. But with such firepower controlling the city, smart criminals found easier targets. The remaining baddies were Mundanes and best dealt with by local police.

Flores patrolled Loon Lake from the sky and reported to Roberto on behalf of the National and City Council. The judge from National had said it himself, right after striking Donna silent so she couldn't protest. Senora Alvarez was a world-renowned expert in dragons. Her son, Roberto, had manipulated Priya, tapping into deep reserves of magic to transform hatchling dragons into adults, a pair that went on to capture swimmers and use their bodies to gestate their eggs.

Once the outside world heard about these seemingly impossible feats, practitioners worldwide yearned to taste Loon Lake's unique power: ancestor magic. The Ashton men had fought against opening Loon Lake Village to outsiders, and so had some members of the Council, but in the end, the judge from National Council overruled them because the secret was out.

Loon Lake could no longer hide from the magical world. They could keep Mundanes from entering Loon Lake Village, but the local cemetery was a wonder of the magic-using world. People from all over yearned to speak to its ghosts, bask in its power, and tap into its phenomenal energy. It was only fair, the Alvarez family insisted, after quietly buying up stores, empty lots, the hotel, and a restaurant. Their empire, started with a single bakery, made them the town's richest business owners. Paloma's clout made Donna jealous and Marvin furious. They had the means and motive.

Tonya moved Paloma and her son to the top of her mental suspect list.

With the ceremony over, the brothers muttered about Paloma's nerve in voices only Tonya could hear. Discreetly, Tonya circled back around the crowd, wondering who else had a motive, when she saw Marta headed her way.

In high school, Tonya would have retreated, so she spoke first to prevent any awkwardness. "I'm sorry for your loss."

Too pale, Marta turned puffy eyes up to Tonya. "Help me."

"Sorry?"

Marta put out a hand to shake and pulled Tonya close enough to whisper. "Someone killed my mother."

"Why do you think that?"

"Bear attack? No bear could have taken down Mom. She was fierce and more powerful than you think. Please, find who did this."

Heaviness collected in Tonya's stomach making it hard to breathe. She clawed her scarf away from her throat. "Why ask me?"

"You found Helen's killer."

"Because I was desperate, and nobody believed I was innocent. You should tell the police."

"They think a bear did it."

"I don't mean the Mundane police." Tonya thumbed at the stranger in the greatcoat, standing a hundred paces behind them. "Do you see that guy with the epaulets on his shoulders? I think he's from National."

"I'd rather pay you."

When Tonya hesitated, Marta said, "Money's not a problem."

"Why ask me when there's an officer right there?" It stung a bit that Marta tried to bribe her.

"I've never asked you for anything." The softness melted from Marta's face, leaving a flinty stare.

Marta delighted in taunting Tonya and excluding her from her Mod peer group. Bullies don't change, and she might turn on her later, but Tonya decided to help.

Before she could offer, Marta spun on her high heels. "I'll remember this!"

She accosted the officer, who didn't seem surprised. With dragon hearing, Tonya discerned every word of Marta's plea for justice and noticed when he looked up at Tonya. Had the stranger overheard Tonya's conversation with Marta? Even for a National rep, he had a strange vibe.

She opened herself to the energy surrounding her. It was risky in the cemetery where so many ghosts held a grudge against her, but she had to know what he was. Slowly, the visible world faded leaving a matrix of fuzzy green dots in the black three-dimensional map in her mind. A large, pulsing dot of energy emanated from each person. The life force of trees, squirrels, beetles, and worms deep in the ground glowed like tiny green balls. Once tapped into the matrix of life, she could use her inner sight to map the glowing balls of energy onto people. Again, she sensed his dark energy, red where everyone else pulsed with healthy green life.

She stopped probing when Ted Kwok, the spry elder who ran the campground, accosted her. "I didn't think I'd ever see you at an Ashton funeral."

Mr. Kwok used to let Tonya hide from Marta and the popular girls in his camp store. When Tonya was particularly upset, he let her sample the candy. It felt weird talking to him adult to adult.

"I wanted to pay my respects like everybody else. How's the rebuild coming?"

That summer, the cabins on Kwok's campground had mysteriously burned down.

"Winter should be slow season, but I can't get labor. Local contractors have too much work, and they've raised their rates."

"Too busy working for the Alvarez family?"

"Yeah. A raceway, the hotel, and a new restaurant next to their bakery." He lowered his voice, since the Alvarez's lingered, chatting with Marvin. "They got the Dougal Mansion rezoned commercial. Must have bribed the historical society to look the other way. Do you know how many businesses have petitioned to restore it?"

"There must be money in cruise ships."

His expression darkened. "For bars and restaurants, but campers want peace and natural beauty. Who'll stay in my campground once it's surrounded by hotels and a noisy racetrack?"

"You could ask City Council to block their building permits."

Kwok lowered his voice. "With Donna gone, maybe. She supported all their new building schemes, even against her brothers Marvin and Stephen. I overheard the three of them yelling at each other."

"What was it about?"

"Marvin said Loon Lake was losing its character, and Stephen couldn't find parking for his Audi TT Roadster."

Good old Mr. Kwok. Heart of gold, ears of platinum. Maybe Hatch was innocent, and Marvin had used Flores to kill Donna. Roberto had Flores trained to help Ashton Security. The leap from that to murder was pretty far, but any possibility that Hatch might be innocent was a straw worth grasping.

"Can you see Flores from the camp office?"

"Rarely. Are you suggesting the dragon burned down my cabins and Caleb's store?"

"National never looked into it, did they? And the judge they sent knew Paloma Alvarez. He called her the dragon expert."

"You're wondering if they took sides." Kwok shrugged. "I appreciate what you're saying, but I trust National. When you leave Loon Lake and visit other magical sites, you'll see how they keep big cities safe and organized. Magic would drown the world in chaos without National."

"So, you don't think it was a dragon or human arson?"

"Just terrible luck. I'm rebuilding the cabins with fireproof interiors."

"Sounds expensive."

"It'll cost a lot more than my insurance covered, but it's okay." He bit his lip. "Too bad my dream of retiring went up with the smoke."

"Oh, Mr. Kwok." That hurt to hear, especially after he'd been so good to Tonya. "That's just terrible." Worse still, he was wrong about it being luck.

Roberto trained Loon Lake's remaining dragon, and Paloma Alvarez was an internationally renowned dragon expert. No way had their beast accidentally burned the campground or killed Donna. If their dragon had committed a crime, it was deliberate. But why?

Kwok's campground was outside Loon Lake Village—prime real estate for magical practitioners. Mayor Ashton had used her clout to support cruise ships and new building projects, making her an ally to the Alvarez family. They had a trained dragon, but no motive for murder.

14

Helen went off on her own while Tonya lingered a while, eavesdropping in the diminishing crowd. She had given up on learning anything more when a deep voice rang out from behind her.

"Tonya Jones?" The outsider stood close enough for Tonya to confirm that his epaulets bore National Council insignia.

"Stop." The order sent a shudder through her body. He spoke too much like the Ashton Security guards who'd told her when to eat, when to wash, and even when to use the toilet in jail. "Don't leave yet."

"Why?"

"You can help with an ongoing investigation."

"Okay..." Had somebody seen her with the body on the beach?

He stroked the hard planes of his chin. "Walk with me?" He put a heavy hand on her shoulder.

She shrugged it off. "I haven't done anything wrong." Except steal a silver ring.

"Then you should cooperate." He walked her uphill from the graveside toward a black sedan parked in the chapel lot.

It seemed like his definition of help with an investigation was a lot different from hers. As they neared the top of the hill, she slowed. "Am I under arrest?"

"That depends on how you answer my questions—and try not to hyperventilate." His smile didn't reach his eyes. "Nobody's hurting you." He reached for her.

"Don't touch me."

"Not as long as you cooperate."

"I want a lawyer."

"Fine, request a witch's advocate when we get to the station—but know this. You gave up the right to protection under Mundane law the first time you used magic."

"Who says I..."

He gave her a withering look. "Nice necro hair."

"That's not fair!" Bringing up her white hair was a low blow. "I never planned this." She gestured at her hair.

"I've seen your file. Where were you the night Donna Ashton died?"

"In my dorm room, trying to sleep. Then I went up to the roof to get some air."

He pressed his lips together, repressing a smile. He knew something but wasn't telling.

"Do you remember anything else?"

"Should I?" The last few mourners passed by, talking softly and stealing glances at them.

"Don't take offense. I'm just doing my job."

"Interesting, because there isn't anyone from National assigned to Loon Lake. This is an independent city with our own bylaws and Ashton Security to back up the Mundane police."

"Get used to me. The local business owners pooled resources to pay my salary, and your City Council approved my position this morning."

"Why?"

"They're nervous. Some of them don't believe a bear killed Donna Ashton."

Tonya tried another angle. "Marta thinks someone murdered her mother and asked me to look into it."

"Why you?"

"No Mundane could overpower Donna, and I don't believe the bear theory either."

"You seem to know a lot about it."

"Small city, smaller community. Marta and I grew up together."

"Share anything relevant."

"What's your name?"

"Sheriff Bjorn Anderson."

That was news to her. "We don't have a sheriff."

"City Council wants me to be the police chief, lead detective, and National Council liaison rolled into one. They let me pick my title." He threaded his thumbs through his belt loops and smiled, making his green eyes sparkle. "Sheriff sounded cool."

He looked thirty, with a tanned face and broad shoulders that strained his coat. It was a body built for hockey or tackling criminals.

"Do you have any theories?" Tonya asked.

"The investigation is ongoing, but if you hear anything, call me." He handed her a business card and left.

Business card for the new sheriff? That was fast, but maybe National print shops ran on the same magic that let their investigators pop out of nowhere. The last time National had interfered in the affairs of Loon Lake, the ruling had gone against the Ashton Family. And Marta had been so insistent that she needed help. With the sheriff on the case, did Tonya need to do anything?

A veil of flurries obscured her dragon vision as she made her way home, still amazed at the frosty smells coming from the pines, the frigid lake, and the snowy path tamped down by passing boots.

Halfway between the cemetery and campus, footsteps made Tonya stop to look back. The mourners had long gone, leaving her alone on the narrow path running parallel to the south shore. Was the sheriff tailing her? Tonya sped up, looked back, slowed down. She sped up again, then turned suddenly and looked over her shoulder.

Nobody.

Tonya reached out and sensed for life force, but either it wasn't there or it was shielded. She'd feel silly if it weren't for the hairs standing on the back of her neck. Maybe a vindictive ghost had followed her out of the cemetery. Not many could leave, so it must be a powerful spirit. She shivered as snow gusted at her back. After burning down the Three-Century-Ash, and half the trees in the cemetery, the ghosts would never forgive her, but they listened to Priya.

As a kindness, Tonya's bestie had set up a meeting with the ghosts who blamed Tonya for burning down the Ash. Talk about a weird and uncomfortable afternoon. Priya had been able to see who Tonya was apologizing to, but the ghosts had stayed invisible. It was their way of snubbing her.

The ghosts had left her alone during the ceremony, probably out of respect for Donna. Tonya almost missed seeing Johnny Scoop, the phantom newsboy who used to tail her everywhere, trying to break a big story. Now that Tonya had fallen out of the spotlight, the ghostly newsboy must have moved on to more newsworthy victims.

Tonya smiled. Maybe he would latch onto the new sheriff.

15

Helen had invited Tonya to her spacious apartment above the new Herbal Healing Shop, but it was a trap. Her birth mom wanted them to attend the wake together.

"It'll be fun." Helen lifted a deep-backed black dress out of her closet and did a little spin.

"Nobody will be happy to see us."

"I know!" Helen spritzed herself with cologne and got changed. "All the Mods will be there. Aren't you curious to see the Ashton's mansion?"

Tonya didn't want to see Marta Ashton, because her classmate's grief and her request for help at the funeral were impossible to resist. There would be no reward for helping Marta, only more suffering for Tonya if she messed things up. The slender diving team diva had bullied her throughout high school because of her height and weight. Now that Tonya was curvy but fit, Marta teased her for losing her powers.

"Why go where we aren't wanted?"

"If I never went where people didn't want me, I'd spend every night at home. Come on, it'll be fun." Helen's eyes sparkled.

The age gap was only nineteen years, and sometimes Helen's hijinks made Tonya feel like the parent. In the end, Tonya decided watching out for Helen inside enemy territory was better than letting her go alone.

"All right, but I'm only going because Marta asked me to find out who killed her mother." The family would keep everything to themselves, but with dragon hearing, she might overhear something juicy.

It wasn't five o'clock yet, but the sun was already setting as they drove west over the River Bridge, not turning south until they neared Loon Lake Village. Protected by cement walls topped with broken glass, the Ashton Family Compound lay just south of the village wall. Tonya admired the glowing lights on the third floor of the mansion. So many windows!

A barrier arm blocked the entrance, and an Ashton Security Guard gestured for them to lower the car window. He frowned at Helen. She got that a lot.

"Were you invited?"

"We attended the funeral. Nobody else needed a formal invitation."

"Wait." The guard picked up a walkie-talkie.

With her dragon hearing, Tonya heard him ask another guard for Marvin Ashton's approval. In the five minutes the guard waited for a reply, cars accumulated behind them until they snaked down the road. Horns honked and people shouted out of their windows. Tonya admired Helen's timing which put maximum pressure on the guard who holstered his walkie-talkie.

"Never mind." Helen held out a black envelope. "Could you pass this condolence card to the Ashtons for us?"

As the guard took the card, Helen put a hand on his arm and made deep eye contact. With a goofy look, he nodded and smiled, his eyes focused on the distance.

"Take it to her yourself, Madame." The barrier rose.

"What if he loses his job?" Tonya asked. "You shouldn't charm the Mundanes!"

"It's the Ashton's fault for employing them. Now relax mini-Barbara, or you'll give yourself wrinkles."

The gleaming white mansion, equipped with Corinthian columns, loomed over a circular driveway. Permanent fixtures highlighted a landscaped front garden with bare maple trees and frozen ornamental cabbages.

Apex predators. Helen pointed to topiary shrubs trimmed to resemble a panther and a tiger. The walkway was flanked by a pair of rising cobras. *As if we needed more proof the Ashtons are psychopaths.*

"No more telepathy. It's rude."

"Maybe you'd be happier waiting in the car."

Helen ignored the parking area and pulled over at the head of the driveway. Not waiting for Tonya, she stepped through the double doors into a two-story entranceway lit by dazzling chandeliers. Beside the door, uniformed staff took Helen's coat into a walk-in cloakroom. Tonya waved them away.

"We're not staying long."

"Speak for yourself." Helen accepted the coat check ticket and swiped two glasses from a passing silver tray.

When Helen handed Tonya a glass of red, she accepted it automatically. She didn't even like wine, but it gave her hands something to do while she tried not to watch Helen enjoying the event. It promised to be a very long and embarrassing night. Tonya loved her birth mom, but the way this crowd stared at them was another reason to escape her hometown. As soon as she could free herself of Hatch and learn to control her powers, she was moving to the city and never looking back.

Dressed in black velvet and a stunning diamond necklace, Marta descended an impressive curved staircase.

Check out those rocks! Hatch wolf-whistled inside Tonya's head.

Calm down. I can't talk to Marta with you distracting me.

Feeble human. He went silent, but she could feel him crouch in a corner of her mind, judging each move.

She needed to question Marta about the mayor's activities on the night she died, but not in front of a crowd. From the entryway, Tonya slipped into the massive dining room lined with tables and glittering with polished silverware.

This brought her into the sphere of Paloma and Victor Alvarez, and their son who looked away as she passed. Unaware of Tonya's superior hearing, Paloma whispered to Roberto to watch Tonya and report back. Could that be who had followed her from the cemetery? He was creepy enough.

The Ashton's peers wore tailored suits and this year's dresses. The Mods used their new right to sell magical services to attract exclusive clientele. Unfamiliar rich folks made up half the attendees. With a nervous glance, Tonya checked for students who might recognize her from the Mackenzie Residence.

Nope. Nothing but Mods and rich outsiders here. Eyes closed, she sensed the energy signatures in the room, confirming it. The outsiders were practitioners, too. No Mundanes at all.

Hatch groaned with excitement. *Look at the gold! The platinum! I wanna go back and touch Marta Ashton's necklace. Get close to her for me.*

Shh. That necklace was her mother's. It was risky to speak to Hatch telepathically in case Helen overheard, but he was losing control.

As the dragon's gold lust rose, Tonya also hungered for treasure. Gleaming precious metals and sparkly stones lured her across the floor to admire the jewels worn by an elegant matron. Pear-shaped diamond earrings caught the chandelier light, casting glittery rainbows on the woman's wrinkled neck. Tonya yearned to caress the sparkling gems.

"Strange girl, stop staring at me!" The woman turned abruptly and stalked away.

Stephen's wearing a Cartier watch. He probably collects more pretties in his bedroom. Let's go upstairs.

"Absolutely not!"

People stared at Tonya.

"What's wrong? Haven't you seen people argue with themselves?" Let them think what they liked. Allies of the Ashtons would never befriend people like her and Helen anyway.

Where had her birth mother gone?

Watching for Helen, Tonya traded her wine glass for a cup of punch and explored beyond the dining room and through a parlor. In a den lined with leather-bound hardbacks, Marvin held court to a circle of well-wishers, but what drew Tonya and Hatch like starving men to a feast was the thick gold-topped staff in his hand.

A grapefruit-sized amethyst glinted atop a crown-shaped gold setting with filigree leaves and roses. Portraits of three witches, maiden, mother, and crone, ran in a circle around the polished wooden staff—which ended in splinters. Something powerful had snapped the Staff of Storms in two.

She remembered the surge of power on the beach. Mayor Ashton would never have returned power to Tonya willingly. Someone had broken the staff, and whoever did it was probably guilty of murder.

"As acting Mayor, let me reassure you that Ashton Security will use the Staff of Storms to enforce City Council's wishes," Marvin promised, "until we can elect a new mayor."

Above the crowd, Tonya said, "It's not working."

Marvin ignored her, choosing to answer a question from the scrum of concerned Mods surrounding him.

This time Tonya shouted. "Is the prison under City Hall still suppressing magic?" From personal experience, she knew the Staff of Storms captured the prisoner's powers so they couldn't charm the guards or magic themselves through the walls.

Stephen parted the crowd in a rush to intercept Tonya. "Take your mother and go home." His red face gleamed with sweat under the glittering chandelier light.

"Why?" Helen stepped out of the crowd. "We both dealt with Donna personally. It's our duty to remember her and share our memories of the real Donna with these newcomers." The glass Helen raised to toast trembled slightly in her hand.

"Stop making a scene." Marvin stared at Tonya until her cheeks heated. "Get your so-called mother out of here."

Tonya took Helen's arm to lend her stability. *Let's just go,* she urged telepathically, turning them away from Marvin.

But Helen was drunk and high on her joy at Donna's demise. *Wait for it. I spiked the punch to loosen people's tongues. I want to find out who starts bragging that they killed Donna, so I can shake their hand.*

Why do you think she was murdered?

Oh pul-ease. There was probably a lineup to see who could kill her first.

At least Tonya and her birth mom wanted to solve the same mystery—but for radically different reasons. She started to lead Helen away so she could snoop around, but Helen turned back, her eyes narrowed at Marvin.

"Where were you the night your sister died?"

Stephen shouted, "He doesn't answer to you!"

With one hand, he grabbed Helen's arm behind her back and marched her toward the door until Marvin stopped him with a hand on his chest.

"I want to answer. My brother and I were here that night. Donna often worked past midnight, so when she was late again, we went to bed."

"You heard him. Now leave." Stephen crooked a finger at a pair of Ashton guards guarding the French doors into the garden.

Before they could leave their posts, Tonya touched Helen's arm. "This is going to be a lot less embarrassing if they don't throw us out." They wove through the crowd until, in the glamorous entryway, Tonya whispered, "How could you?"

"Just trying to help."

As if. Tonya did her coat up so fast her hands fumbled the buttons. When she finished, she spotted Helen dart back into the dining room.

Tonya went after her, but Marvin took Tonya's arm and steered her into the kitchen, noisy with banging, sizzling, and chopping. He whispered in her ear, "Don't tell people the Staff of Storms doesn't work."

"Donna took my powers with the Staff in the summer, but they came back to me when she died."

"You're wrong." His expression was granite.

"Marta suspects a supernatural creature killed her."

"Helen charms animals, she hated Donna, and now she's at the wake to rub it in." Marvin wasn't whispering anymore. "She killed my sister!"

"No. Helen's immature but innocent."

"She better leave before Stephen catches her."

"Or what? He'll put her into a coma?" *Like he'd done to Mayor Thornton.* "At his own sister's wake?"

"You're right. Stephen won't lose it with so many people around—probably."

But Tonya couldn't let go of her questions. "Donna must have been carrying the staff with her the night she died. The dragon saw all that beautiful gold and killed her for it."

"What dragon?"

"I don't believe it was a bear, do you?" It was a stupid slip, probably brought on by drinking Helen's truth punch. Tonya put her hands over her mouth. She didn't feel drunk or wobbly, just loose. Better keep her mouth shut until it wore off. "I know the Staff of Storms doesn't work." *Crud!*

Hatch's laughter echoed in her mind.

Marvin glanced at the busy kitchen staff. Almost as tall as his brother, he looked down into Tonya's eyes. "What I tell you doesn't get repeated."

"Okay..."

"The Staff of Storms is a prop without magic."

Steal it for me, Hatch commanded.

"But Donna used it to strip my abilities. It created the anti-magic field around the jail."

"It only seemed that way. Donna did it herself."

"How? She never had powers."

"That's what we let people think. My sister spent her life faking weakness."

"I don't believe you," she goaded to keep him talking.

"Donna could capture and use other witch's powers, but if outsiders knew, they would have killed her to protect themselves or kidnapped her to make her teach them how to do it."

Poor Donna. How terrible to grow up poor and despised for weakness, all the time knowing that if you used your strength, power-mad witches might kill you. "Why are you telling me this?"

"We're in a crisis without Donna's powers to keep practitioners in the jail or take the powers of irate visitors. You're smart, and I can see you figuring it out, but I'm appealing to you as an Old Family member—don't tell anyone."

Stephen joined them, accompanied by two Ashton guards escorting Helen. His voice rumbled, "You control animals." He pointed at Helen. "You hated Donna." He poked Tonya's shoulder. "And now you've come to laugh at her wake? Nice confession, idiots."

He ordered the guards, "Put them in a van and deliver them to the sheriff."

As Stephen and his guards led Helen back to the entranceway, Tonya appealed to Marvin. "Helen didn't do anything to Donna."

"To hurt our family," Stephen said, "there's nothing she wouldn't do."

Marta joined her uncles to pile it on. "Mom was Helen's biggest enemy."

Hit her! Hit her! Hatch wouldn't be happy until Tonya hurt Marta, but he would have to be satisfied with talking.

"My. Mother. Didn't. Kill. Anyone!" It felt so good to yell right in Marta's face.

Helen's punch must have erased her inhibitions, because Marta swatted at Tonya, who danced away.

Suddenly, the sheriff threw open the doors and ordered the guards to escort Helen into an Ashton security van that was waiting in the drive.

How did Anderson know to arrive at that precise moment?

There was little time to ponder, because Ashton guards grabbed Tonya by the arms and marched her out to join Helen in the van.

16

HANDCUFFED TO BENCHES AND facing each other from opposite sides of the van, Tonya and Helen sat in the dark. The gravel road jolted Tonya, reminding her of another bumpy journey in an identical Ashton Security van—driving her to a magic-proof cell under City Hall. When she finally escaped Loon Lake, she was never coming back.

"Where are they taking us?" she whispered to Helen. "Magic prison can't hold you without Donna's powers."

"Who says I'd try to break out?"

The Ashton van's ability to deaden magic had also ended with Donna. Despite the thick metal encasing them, Tonya sensed glowing green life force coming from the driver. Beside him, a pulsing mass of red energy.

Weird. Life force in people, animals, and plants typically manifested as pulsing green light. Death energy, linked to necromancy, was black-on-black and absorbed life force like a mystical black hole.

But red energy? She'd only felt that once before.

Fifteen minutes later, the van slowed onto the gravel shoulder. The terrain under the wheels turned spongy as they rolled a little farther, then stopped.

Helen's bright green energy shifted in the dark. "Where are we?"

"I can't sense much through a metal van, but it's too quiet for town." At this hour, Loon Lake streets would be full of holiday traffic. In Loon Lake Village, cruise ship revelers would be shouting, slinging spells, and staggering through the streets leaving trash and spent magic behind.

Weight shifted, tilting the van, and the front doors slammed.

The driver flung open the back doors, revealing a round red pavilion glowing against the nighttime forest. From her spot chained to the bench, Tonya estimated the side walls at eight feet tall with a center pole twice that height.

"Are we going to the circus?"

The driver blinded Tonya with a high-powered flashlight aimed at her face. Behind him, Anderson said, "I'll take it from here."

The security guard drew Anderson aside, but Tonya's acute hearing deciphered every whisper. "Helen can influence your mind, and Tonya can suck life force until your empty husk blows away on the breeze. Are you sure you don't want backup?"

"It's under control." Anderson walked the guard back to the doors. "Do me the honor?"

The guard clambered into the van and uncuffed them from the benches. He stood back as Sheriff Anderson handed Helen out of the van. When the sheriff's hand touched Tonya's, a shiver crossed her back. What secret powers fed this man's attitude?

The driver looked from Tonya to the big tent and back at Anderson. "You're good?"

"Enjoy your evening." Anderson contemplated the moon as the guard got into the van and drove away.

Once the taillights faded in the distance, Anderson led them to the pavilion. Helen stayed silent. Not one telepathic barb or whispered joke.

"Don't worry," Tonya whispered. "You didn't do it, so they can't prove you did."

Helen nudged Tonya. "How would you know?"

Anderson stopped at the entrance. "What you're about to see must remain secret."

"You're relying on my honor as a criminal?" Helen raised a pale eyebrow, her face and white hair tinted red by the pavilion's glow.

"Honor among thieves," he chuckled. Through the tent flap, he revealed an impossibly large space with walls and ceiling tiles at right angles that didn't correspond even slightly to the tent's exterior. The décor featured beige walls, drab landscape prints, and the kind of sturdy office furniture that grows on cubicle farms.

Behind a chipped counter, a cop wearing the National Council uniform waved them through to a bullpen as wide as a football field. On all sides, desktops disappeared under phones, computers, and stacks of files. Suit-and-badge types leaned back in swivel chairs, reading papers or hunched over their desks making notes. This frenetic activity extended into the distance where other bullpens full of different detectives worked cases from myriad locations around the world. There were so many that distance blurred the details of the farthest work areas, tinting them blue with mist, like faraway mountains.

Closer to Tonya, at crooked rows of battered desks, officers wearing a wide international selection of Mundane uniforms testified to detectives in suits.

"What is this place?" Tonya asked.

"The tent is a moving gateway to National's central police station." He gestured at the innumerable bullpens ahead of them, fading to a point on the distant horizon.

"Are there more gateways?" she asked.

He nodded.

"Which explains how you got here so fast."

Trailing behind them, Helen didn't comment.

Holding cells occupied a side wall so long that perspective shrank it to a point. Closer at hand, glassed-in offices with drawn blinds punctuated the floor space.

Anderson stopped. "This is it."

They stood in the middle of a bullpen where human and humanoid detectives were interspersed with creatures of legend and nightmare.

Tonya knew plenty of witches, and she'd seen more than enough dragons, but werewolves in uniform? Raven informants? Cephalopod cops typing with tentacles?

A chic woman in black pierced Tonya with her gaze. She had such a symmetrical face, pale with ashy shadows under the eyes. Tonya's feet wouldn't move, and she couldn't break eye contact. Heart fluttering and breathing too fast, she whispered, "Is that a vampire?"

"Yes, and *she* has excellent hearing." The cop smiled, revealing her fangs.

When the vampire resumed chatting with a black leather-clad warrior woman, Tonya could finally look away but nearly tripped over a turtle-man moseying across her path.

"Wait here while I interrogate Helen." Anderson pointed to a nearby chair.

"Please don't leave me here." With her back to the vampire, Tonya used two fingers to mimic fangs.

Anderson gave her a long, hard look.

"Please." Even in her own ears, Tonya's voice sounded pathetic.

"All right." Leaving the bullpen behind, he led them to a corridor lined with interrogation rooms. "Wait out here."

After Helen took her seat at the table, Anderson went to shut off the camera. "Don't disturb us." He shut the door in Tonya's face.

"You can't hold me," Helen protested loudly. "I'm innocent!"

"Stop resisting and answer my questions!" Anderson's voice boomed through the door.

The loud interrogation continued for a bit, but then their voices faded to whispers. What were they saying?

A door and a wall would stop a normal human, but Tonya's dragon senses deciphered every whisper.

Softly, Anderson chuckled. "I apologize for bringing you in."

"The party was starting to bore me anyway."

Helen was joking around with him! She hadn't reacted to seeing the vampire either.

"How are the Ashtons handling City Council without Donna?"

"Stephen's full of bluster, but he ran out of the emergency meeting in tears."

"And Marvin?"

"He's a cool fish," Helen said. "He only cares about efficiency, logistics, and money."

"Is Council restless?"

"It's too soon to tell. Marvin supports the new status quo, but Stephen wants to run against him in the by-election."

Tonya had heard enough. She thrust open the door. "You're working for him!"

Helen didn't even look guilty. "National needs information."

"Is that why the judge found you innocent? Because you're their spy?"

"No, honey. You proved my innocence, or National would have made me disappear."

Helen tried to pull her into a hug, but Tonya resisted. They stood together for an awkward moment.

"Then why?"

"The Trads ran me out of town at the age of nineteen." Helen's brow creased at the memory. "Did you want me to starve, live like a street kid?"

It was the one topic Helen never discussed. She'd left Loon Lake pregnant with Tonya, alone and without allies. Mom liked to brag how she tracked Helen to a tiny room in a rundown hotel and dragged her sister back to live with her—but Barbara had never specified a timeline. National must have given her a job before her sister came for her.

Helen put a hand to her waist and cocked her hip. "Am I free to go?"

"I'll get an unmarked car to drop you off."

"I'm coming too." This place creeped Tonya out.

"You stay." Anderson's expression was dead serious.

"Helen, stay with me." She couldn't believe her birth mom didn't care.

Helen shared a look with Anderson. "She won't need me if she's innocent."

"If? You think I did something?"

Helen deadpanned. "Don't you?"

That hurt. Tonya had risked her life for Helen. If she thought her own daughter was guilty, Anderson probably thought so too. Even Tonya had her doubts, but she'd never know the truth if they put her in a cell. Only she could find out what happened that night—if Hatch would come clean instead of fighting her tooth and claw.

After Helen left, Tonya said, "I want a witch's advocate."

"No, you don't." Anderson's voice went soft. "Bring in an advocate, and I'll have to charge you to keep you here."

National would do the expedient thing—without concern for local needs. It was one reason Mayor Thornton had fought so hard to keep Loon Lake independent from the outside magical world.

Anderson invited Tonya to sit across from him. She stared at the restraint rings built into the table while he switched on a wall-mounted camera. "Mind if I record your testimony as a witness?"

Tonya shrugged. "I have nothing to hide."

That triggered a half smile as he sat across from her, hands folded on the table. "The Old Families view you according to their factions. They either hate or love you, but I don't care about politics." He leaned forward, sending tremors through his massive arms. "I want your alibi. Where were you the night Mayor Ashton died?"

"Sleeping in the Mackenzie dorm."

"Can anyone vouch for you?"

"I don't have a roommate, but I watched some TV in the common room. Someone might have seen me go in or out of the shower room."

It was weird. The longer he questioned her, the more Anderson drew her in. It wasn't the big shoulders or the angle of his square jaw, but she couldn't forget the magical shock when he touched her hand. Why did she yearn to close the distance between them when she should feel scared? Was he a vampire too, using his glamor to charm her? It was rude to ask and dumb to provoke a detective, but she had to know. She leaned forward and took a whiff.

The sheriff didn't smell of herbs and garlic like a witch. His minty cologne enveloped her with a hint of burned sugar.

Anderson sat back, crossing his muscled arms with a bemused smile. "Are you finished sniffing me?"

"It's not fair. You know everything about me, but I don't even know what you are."

"I'm the one asking questions. What's the rest of your alibi?"

"That's it. I went to bed." Then Hatch had taken over doing who knew what mischief until she awoke at the edge of the beach near Donna's body. No amount of searching her memory could dredge up what she'd done as a dragon, but when she stumbled over the corpse, the nearby sand had smelled sweet and minty. Could it have been Anderson's cologne?

"When did you wake up?"

"I don't know." She tried to remember if wild mint grew near that section of the beach. If the detective had arrived before she woke up and looked around long enough to leave traces of cologne on the scene, he already knew the answers. He was toying with her, letting Tonya play out enough yarn to tangle herself up—unless he'd killed Donna and was looking to make her the patsy.

"Are you sure that's it?"

Her mind had wandered. "Sorry."

Anderson narrowed his eyes. "Things will go better for you if you tell the whole truth."

Tonya let his threat hang without reacting, but Hatch gave a silent roar.

Nice one. Look at you all brave and defiant! What did you do with puny Tonya?

Anderson's expression softened. "Please say you were with a lover, or there's another dragon you're protecting."

He knew about Hatch? Did Helen know? She kept her voice steady. "What dragon?"

"Please. You tell me, because you're the prime suspect until you can prove your innocence."

Tonya crossed her arms, thankful he hadn't cuffed her to the table. He knew she was lying, so she had to make him trust her, at least until she could discover the truth. If treasure-hungry Hatch had killed Donna fighting over the Staff of Storms, she would face the consequences; but if he was setting her up, she needed to get away.

"I slept on the beach, and I did see the body. It looked like a dragon slashed it open."

"Finally, an ounce of truth."

"Maybe you should talk to Roberto Alvarez and his mother, Paloma. They're the dragon specialists."

"Duly noted. What else aren't you telling me?"

"Since Donna Ashton became mayor, the Alvarez family has fought to control City Council. Donna opposed the magic tourists, but Paloma won over the business owners' association—after she bought up half of Loon Lake Village."

"Don't deflect. What else did you see on the beach?" He leaned on the table, revealing an ashy, masculine scent under his menthol cologne.

Scales and brimstone! Could he be?

"I've been very patient, but if you don't cooperate..."

"You'll huff and you'll puff, and you'll burn my house down?"

"Took you long enough."

"You're the first other person I've met with a dragon inside. How did you get yours?"

The sheriff's eyes widened. "Are you only a dragon on your father's side?"

"I don't understand."

With a reptilian stare, he said, "I have you on camera, naked, breaking into a marina building. Later, you come out wearing sweats. I think you got rid of the clothes because they were covered in Donna's blood."

"I found her, but I didn't kill her."

"You've done nothing but lie to me. Why should I believe you?"

"I didn't think you'd believe I have a dragon inside me."

"Try me." He leaned across the table and inhaled luxuriously, allowing her to see his expression of pleasure, as if savoring exquisite perfume.

"Stop sniffing me!"

"But it's so good and such a rare treat. Not counting my mother, it's been ten years since I've smelled a dragon-woman."

"I'm not a dragon-woman."

"I watched you take off from the roof of your building."

"You've been spying on me!"

"Helen too. We're very concerned about you." He leaned back into his chair. "Did you kill Donna Ashton?"

Emotions tangled up logic with him leaning in close, smelling ashy, exciting, and strangely familiar. Heavy gold chains peeked out of his collar and cuffs, and the large emerald on his finger triggered her gem lust.

"I didn't kill anyone, but there is a dragon inside me called Hatch. In the summer, he was an infant, satisfied to ride along and take telepathic swipes at me, but he's maturing fast and trying to take over."

Anderson raised his eyebrows but didn't interrupt as the rest spilled out of her. "The night of the murder, he forced me to shift into dragon form. I blacked out and don't remember anything until I woke in the woods at the edge of the beach."

Silence stretched between them as the sheriff clenched and unclenched his jaw. "I can't ignore that confession. You call yourself Hatch?"

"Hatch isn't me. He's a parasite."

"If you're a shifter, your dragon is you."

"Shifter like shapeshifter?" She cocked her head. "Do you turn into a dragon at the full moon like a werewolf?

"Of course not."

"How am I supposed to know how it works? I wasn't born like this. A mother dragon slashed my belly and implanted her egg, which hatched in my gut and started eating me."

"Impossible." Sheriff Anderson braced his fists on the table.

"Ask Helen. My friends and I rescued a handful of tourists from the female dragon's cave on Grand Island."

"You mean Flores."

"We aren't on speaking terms. She attacked swimmers, planted her eggs in them, and buried them alive. They would have died if my friends and I hadn't rescued them. When our boat reached the beach, my powers came back, and I sterilized the eggs."

He leaped to his feet, vibrating with energy. "You killed baby dragons?"

"I had no choice. The people would have died horribly when the eggs hatched and the creatures inside ate their guts."

"So you killed these creatures." His eyebrows knit over a craggy brow. "Anything else you'd care to confess?"

"Before I could deal with my egg, Donna took my powers and turned them against me."

"She drew out your life energy?"

"Worse. She redirected it into the egg, making it mature rapidly. The hatchling broke out of its shell and started chewing through my core."

"Donna didn't take your powers." His lip curled in disgust. "You probed my energy in the van."

"My powers returned when Donna died. The Ashtons lied to protect Donna. The Staff of Storms never siphoned off my powers. She did."

Anderson's arms rippled as he spread his hands. "If you couldn't kill Hatch, then why aren't you dead?"

"On the verge of passing out, I made him a deal to share my body, and that magical contract made us one. For a long time, he was just an annoying voice in my head, but he's getting smarter. He sees everything I see. Knows everything I know ... why can't I hear him thinking?"

"Don't ask me. Born shifter, remember?"

"You see my problem. I didn't willingly kill anybody, but Hatch loves gems. There's a small chance he noticed the Staff of Storms and killed Donna for it."

"It's a believable excuse, but I talked to a local jeweler. You walked out of his store with a ring in broad daylight, and you hadn't shifted. This dragon egg story is unbelievable—a ridiculous excuse for bad behavior. You were on the beach. You disposed of the clothes. You got close enough to the corpse to smell dragon on it. Why didn't you report finding the body?"

"Hatch sometimes takes control. He makes me hunt animals and eat them. Every time I see gold or jewels, I want to steal them." Tonya trembled, her face hot with the rush of blood pulsing in her ears. "Can you make him stop?"

"No."

"Then arrest me. If you're sure I did it, put me in a cell so tight Hatch can't shift without breaking his wings."

17

Roberto stood at the pier on Grand Island watching the lights of his parents' motor launch approach. The white boat, gleaming under the moonlight, and the warm glow of the captain's cabin lights contrasted sharply against the black water. Papi drove while Mami sat in the back, arms folded, her black crocheted shawl flapping in the wind. Mami couldn't swim and hated the water, but away from the bustle in the Condor Bakery, Papi soothed his nerves with fishing. Who could blame him?

One lonely light on a wooden pole illuminated the vessel growling to a stop alongside the pier. With economical gestures, Roberto tied it up with nylon rope.

Mami proffered her hand like the Queen of Spain and waited for Roberto to steady her. With her full skirt held in one hand, she stepped onto the dock. She said in Spanish, "You could have brought the dragon to me."

"This time of night, she's probably in the lake fishing."

"Make tea. I have an important project for you." Mami looked back at Papi, lingering behind the wheel, probably trolling for bass in his daydreams.

"Come along, Victor."

The shrill pitch of her voice jerked Papi to attention, and Roberto led his parents along the modest public beach. Walking close to the waterline on firm sand, it took fifteen minutes to reach the enormous pavilion where he lived and worked with Flores. Dragons remained hatchlings for a month and imprinted on their trainers like geese, but Priya's lightning magic had sped Flores and her dead mate from hatchlings to flame-throwing monsters in weeks. The results delighted Mami, but she didn't have to live in a tent like Roberto, wary that Flores might ambush him someday and barbecue his exquisite surfer's body.

Roberto sat opposite Mami across a folding card table on the sandy ground. She looked from the towering pavilion to his quarters, marked off from Flores' area by a pair of standing privacy curtains. She frowned at the camp sink full of dirty dishes that spread across the folding table he used as a kitchen counter.

What did she expect? When she had moved him onto the island, she should have provided a cleaning service like back home in Lima. Did Mami clean their three-story mansion in Loon Lake Village?

Not a chance, so he didn't see why he couldn't get help here, but Roberto knew better than to complain when Mami was in a mood.

"Tea?" She drummed her fingers on the vinyl tabletop.

Mami enjoyed being waited on. If he objected, she would rant about the pain of childbirth and declare he owed her everything for bringing him into the world. It was easier to fire up the Coleman stove and bend his neck over the dented aluminum kettle.

He returned to the table with three camp mugs and a bowl of sugar cubes for Papi who stood outside the pavilion, his eyes on the lake where the moonlight sparkled on the black water.

"Watch Tonya. Chum with her friend, Priya, to make it look natural."

"Priya won't talk to me." Especially after he romanced her and manipulated her magic.

"Then get really close to Tonya."

"She has a boyfriend."

"You're more handsome and mature than these Canadian hicks. No excuses." Her toothy smile reminded Roberto of Flores. "Bring me the girl to examine once she trusts you."

There was no sense arguing. Mami would never understand that her strong, handsome son could fail at anything. But he'd messed up and almost gotten Lynette killed last Halloween. After distorting Priya's magic to grow Mami's dragons, Tonya and her friends shunned him. He would not make a fool of himself trying to date Tonya.

"Paloma," his father ducked through the tent flap, "isn't it enough our son camps on the island training your creature?"

"The girl harbors Flores' egg. It must mature."

"Even if it kills her?" Roberto turned his back to put his mug in the sink. "At the trial, she said she had a dragon inside her, not a hatchling. How is that possible?"

Mami stood and handed him her cup. "She's not human anymore. The girl has bonded with the dragon."

That made no sense to Roberto. "A dragon shifter is born from dragon parents."

"In the outside world, but in Loon Lake, with converging ley lines and the right conditions, something unique occurred. I must work out how to repeat this. People will give anything to transform into dragons and live for centuries. It's the Fountain of Youth."

"You're crazy."

"Like a fox." Papi allowed himself a small smile.

"Win her over or drag her into my lab, I don't care." Mami thrust open the tent flap. Teatime was over.

He watched Mami labor across the sand into the pool of light by the pier, and his stomach twisted. Once Mami latched onto an idea, there was no shirking. There was a chance Tonya would suffer less if Roberto brought her in himself, alive and willing to explain how she'd combined with the dragon. If the way Tonya told her story captivated Mami, she might escape vivisection.

18

"I won't hold you. For now." The detective fiddled with the camera. "The magical realm doesn't respect Mundane precepts like innocent until proven guilty. If National arrests you, they will treat you as guilty until proven innocent."

Tonya's heart leaped. "Thank you." She could go!

Tonya used to think the worst thing that could happen was spending the rest of her life judged and abused by Loon Lakers who hated her. But no matter how much she yearned for Anderson to set her free, she wanted to prevent another murder even more. "What if Hatch killed Donna, and he kills again?"

"From now on, I'll be watching you closely and so will Helen." He ushered her out. "This isn't over. While I verify the facts, you have four days to find someone who saw you and get a real alibi together, or I'll have to arrest you and put you in a National cell."

"For how long?"

"I'm supposed to say until your trial." He crossed his arms. "Realistically?" He cleared his throat. "National is used to entities with extended lifespans."

"What's that mean?"

"Innocent or not, once National throws you in their cells, Hatch will never fly again."

When Tonya returned to the Mackenzie residence, Priya sat on the battered corduroy sofa in the common room with her brows knit and her arms crossed. "What happened to you?"

"I'm so sorry." They were supposed to meet the Ninjas after Tonya returned from the wake, but it was late by the time Helen picked her up and dropped her home after her inquisition with Anderson. Tonya flopped onto the battered couch beside Priya feeling the wooden frame dig into her legs. "I don't know what to do."

"What's wrong?"

They sat side by side, Tonya facing the blank TV until she summoned the strength to begin. "National interrogated me."

"But they let you go, so everything's okay?"

If she could prove somebody else killed the mayor. Tonya stood. "I need to change clothes. Tell the Ninjas I'm too busy."

Priya followed Tonya to her room. "Why?"

After she closed the door behind them, Tonya told Priya everything. Hatch taking over her body. The blackouts. Waking up on the beach.

"Oh, Tonya." She put a comforting hand on Tonya's shoulder. "What are you going to do?"

"Sheriff Anderson ordered me to prove my innocence, and if I can't find an alibi, they'll jail me forever. The trouble is there can't be an alibi, because if anyone saw me, they know I was there."

"I don't like to ask," Priya glanced down, "but are you sure you weren't involved somehow?"

"I don't trust Hatch. Normally he's always sniping at me, mocking everything I do, but since the mayor died..."

"What is it?"

"He's gone awfully quiet." Tonya felt a comforting squeeze on her shoulder and almost broke down. "That monster is planning something terrible. I feel it."

"I'll tell the others you can't come." Priya dusted her hands together, the same gesture she used to start art projects, finish homework, and tackle life's problems. In the short time she'd known about magic, Priya had learned to bend its energy through her art and see ghosts. She even worked with the terrifying—to Tonya—ghost librarian of City Hall.

This was the worst time to let Priya go. She was Tonya's rock in a world that battered and belittled her.

"I change my mind. Don't leave me alone with Hatch!" This trip to the movies might be her last breath of freedom with the Digital Ninjas before they put her away. "Promise not to tell the others."

"Not even Drake?"

"Especially not him. He tells Zain everything, and Zain..."

"Loves to broadcast everything he knows the minute he knows it. Right, but tell Drake. He loves you. He'll keep your secret."

"He's a Mundane which makes him too vulnerable. I can only tell you. Promise you'll keep my secret?"

"Of course."

Her bestie would never spill, but Tonya felt a lot less confident in herself. The minute she saw Drake and the others, she feared bursting into tears she couldn't explain.

19

It was 9:00 p.m. by the time Tonya and Priya went down to the cafeteria where Zain and Grace were debating which film to see. As they neared the table, Zain put down his hot chocolate and marched to meet her.

"Finally, you deign to join us." For once he wasn't smiling.

"Sorry." Tonya tried not to lie. "Helen dragged me to the wake, and I got delayed." And joining her friends was probably a mistake, a tempting mistake. "I wouldn't blame you if you went without me."

"Don't be silly." Grace handed Tonya an envelope with a candy cane taped to it. "Merry almost Christmas."

It was a cute card featuring a snowman wearing a grass skirt, floral lei, and a Hawaiian shirt. The caption read: Peace, Love, and Pineapples. "Zain helped me choose it, but I added the candy cane."

Zain made a hurry up gesture. "Very nice, season's greetings, but more importantly, what film are we seeing?"

When she didn't respond immediately, Zain tapped his chest. "Let the expert choose."

"What about Drake?" Priya took Zain's hand. "He'll pick something I actually want to see."

Tonya waved hello to Drake who hadn't got up from the table. She walked past Priya to whisper, "I thought you were in Toronto selling cameras."

"I have the evening off. Do you mind?"

Ouch. "Let's watch something fun and Christmassy." A condemned woman's last movie.

"No sappy romances." Grace adjusted a gold hoop earring. "Let's see a classic."

"*Home Alone?*" Drake perked up.

"I am not watching that again," Zain protested. "I watched it 100 times in grade school."

Drake grinned. "We should do Bruce Willis Christmas. *Die Hard*!"

"Woot, woot!" Zain shouted. The guys high-fived each other.

"Exactly how do guns and kidnappers put us in the Christmas spirit?" Grace asked.

"It's about a lonely man trying to reconnect with his ex during the holidays." Zain grinned. "Plus, they trash lots of Christmas merchandise."

Priya curled a braid around her finger. "We can see an action movie any time. This should be special." She glanced at Tonya. "I vote for an art film from Europe or Quebec."

Grace groaned. "Nothing depressing. The classic choice has to be *Christmas Carol* with Alister Sims." She mentioned that film a lot since she'd played Scrooge in a campus production.

"Dull," Zain said, "unless Grace is playing the lead." He glanced at his girl-friend, who blew him a kiss.

"Compromise." Tonya's favorite was old. "Bill Murray in *Scrooged* is classic and funny."

Drake nodded, and Zain scowled but didn't veto the film.

"I've heard it's good." Grace shrugged. "But it's not playing at the cinema."

"Use my streaming account. I have microwave popcorn, and we can order pizza." Tonya wanted to make her last night with friends memorable.

"I second staying in," Zain said. "But we should watch *The Nightmare Before Christmas*."

"Isn't that a cartoon?" Grace asked.

"It's an animated musical feature directed by celebrated auteur Tim Burton." Zain sniffed. "You call yourself an actor?"

"This is going to be another creepy movie, isn't it?" Grace crossed her arms. "Suspense is cool, but I am not watching a horror film at Christmas. Have some respect."

"Don't worry. It's a kid's flick that grownups like." Drake searched for the movie on his phone and showed her the poster. "Jack Skellington, King of Halloween Town, is jealous of Santa and wants to run Christmas Town. Give it ten minutes, and if you hate it, we'll pick something else."

They bought sodas from the cafeteria and piled into the elevator. The common room had a kitchenette on one end where Tonya microwaved popcorn while Drake ordered pizza. Once everybody had settled with their bags of buttery goodness, Zain turned out the lights. Priya relaxed in an easy chair with her feet up, and Zain joined Grace on a couch to one side, leaving Tonya and Drake the lumpy loveseat in the middle. Tonya shifted away from Drake, and so they sat, not touching or speaking, with their eyes aimed at the screen.

A few students from the dorm joined them, laughing at the jokes and heightening the communal experience for Tonya. The odd film, with its quirky romance between Jack the Pumpkin King and Sally, his Bride-of-Frankenstein girlfriend, resonated with Tonya. She too loved hopelessly, trapped in a monstrous patchwork body.

Boring. Why do humans love sitting around?

Tonya hoped if she ignored Hatch, he would leave her alone.

The smell of popcorn is making me hungry. Time to hunt!

No. Tonya needed this fleeting happiness, united with her friends before the sheriff took her away.

Drake whispered, "Is everything okay?"

"Yeah. Don't stop the movie for me. I'll be right back." Maybe she could talk down Hatch in her room.

Halfway down the hall, pain spiked through her body. *No! You can't do this to me here.*

Try and stop me, puny human.

Priya called after Tonya. "Where are you going?"

"Fresh...air." Tonya gasped between waves of pain. If she didn't flee, Hatch would transform her in front of everybody.

"I'll come with," Priya said.

"No." Agony filled her body as organs and bones moved. Tonya stumbled to the end of the hallway and through an emergency exit that led to the roof. She took the stairs two at a time. "Slow down! If I change here, we'll get stuck."

Hurry, then. Once the change starts, you can't stop it. He cackled.

More than once Tonya had wanted to punch his face or douse him with a bucket of ice water, anything to make him suffer a fraction of the pain he inflicted during transformation. But the snickering dragon never suffered. He could pull back into his consciousness when he wished or fully inhabit her mind and sensations at will.

It was the reason she and Drake hadn't done more than hold hands since the summer. She couldn't share her love with a monster, and despite all his love and loyalty, Drake was losing patience. Her frequent disappearances troubled him, but the worst was the way his face crumpled when she pushed him away. She hid her tears because the stakes were bigger than happiness. It was better to lose her love than risk Drake figuring out what was happening and putting himself in the way of Hatch's wrath.

Tonya stumbled, the pain so intense it doubled her over and stole her voice. She wanted to scream—and roar. Her body swelled and her skin stretched. Wings pierced her scaly skin as they emerged from her back, growing and unfurling. Tonya was a passenger in her body as Hatch trotted to the edge of the roof, claws clicking and scraping the gravel.

A glimpse of the flowerbeds below twisted Tonya's stomach, but the scream never passed her scaly lips. Hatch spread their wings and launched them into the night, flapping hard to rise above the tree line. Reaching the clouds, he turned lazy circles above Loon Lake Village, revealing a dizzying view of nighttime revelers below. Inside the wall, purple and green flames erupted from clouds of billowing smoke as practitioners cast flashy spells.

To tame her vertigo, Tonya took slow breaths, but it was too much. She closed her eyes against the roller coaster of rises and dips. Now and then, she risked a peek to track their progress as they left Loon Lake Village behind.

At anchor near the pier, the white cruise ship glowed against black water. Hatch landed at the far end of the public beach near the boat rental, his claws sinking into the sand. He sniffed at the ground like a killer returning to the scene of the crime. Was that what he was doing? Trying to erase trace evidence? Gloating about what he'd made her do? One thing was certain. Hatch's scent already covered this patch of beach.

Telepathically she demanded, *Did you kill Mayor Ashton?*

No response.

Hatch heard her — he could hear all her thoughts — but once he took charge of their form, Hatch didn't care about Tonya's thoughts and feelings anymore. He owned this body that craved the hunt and lusted for gold. The day he got complete control, his dragon form would triumph, and Tonya would never speak or walk on two legs again. So what was Hatch doing, pacing up and down this part of the beach like guilt tormented him? He'd never shown remorse before.

And what was that smell? When Tonya examined this site as a human, she thought her heightened senses had detected everything. Apparently, odors revealed greater complexity to her in dragon form.

A whiff of brimstone clung to the sand where the body had rolled onto the shore, but she also detected the cool top note of expensive aftershave. Did that mean there was another suspect, a man whose hobbies included burning sulfur, personal grooming, and murder?

It made her wonder about Roberto Alvarez. Flores could have killed Donna on his command. Tonya had liked the smell of his icy cologne in first year, when he was dating her roommate, Lynette. That made him a strong suspect, but not the only one. Helen preferred wearing men's cologne.

Roberto was arrogant and entitled, and Helen was powerful and impetuous. Both of them could influence a dragon, but had they made it kill?

20

At midnight, Marta lay in bed thinking about her mother and all the terrible things she wanted to do to the person who had killed her. A chime from the security system alerted her to someone near the side door.

Who would come to that door? And how did they pass the front gate without speaking to the guard?

Her husky brothers should confront whoever it was, and they would have heard the warning sound too. It rang out again, but when she checked her phone app, whoever it was stood outside the view of the fisheye camera lens. That had to be deliberate.

She sat up in bed and shouted, "Answer the door!" But neither of her uncles answered. Stephen had probably gone straight from the gym to his favorite pub in Loon Lake Village, but Marvin would be home.

"Get the door! I'm not dressed." No doubt Marvin was at the computer pretending to do the accounting. Since Mom died, he locked himself in the home office most of the time and barely talked to her or Stephen.

Marta got up, threw a bathrobe over her silk pajamas, and bounced down the grand staircase, but the sound wasn't coming from the main entrance.

Marta detoured through the formal dining room and parlor to the former kitchen they used as a pantry just as the knuckle rapping sound changed to boots kicking. Feminine shouts penetrated the door as Marta wrenched it open.

"Yes?"

A gaunt woman in a long nylon coat smiled, revealing yellowed teeth and receding gums. A dusting of snow clung to her messy gray hair which radiated an eerie light.

"How did you get past security?" A high cement wall surrounded the family compound, and guards watched the gate around the clock.

The glowing phantom pursed her lips. "Don't you know me, Thumbelina?"

"Grandma?" Marta hated that pet name, inspired by her tiny size at birth.

"There's my girl."

Grandma opened her arms and tried to hug her, but Marta propped her foot against the door, speaking through the crack. "Where did you come from?" It was a loaded question, since Grandma was not one of the regular ghosts in the Loon Lake Cemetery.

"That story would make a great movie, but I can't tell it on the doorstep. Let your old grandma in?"

Chilly wind gusted snowflakes at Marta's face, but she hesitated. A tough character, Grandma Ashton had disciplined Marta's mother with a wooden spoon. Her rivals suffered crop failures, sick livestock, and a sadistic array of misfortunes. It was exactly the type of personality to spawn a vengeful ghost.

"Promise you're not here to hurt anybody."

Grandma sailed through the door and hovered above the red tile floor.

Marta stumbled backward. "What do you want?"

"Wendel's coming, and there's been some unpleasant tittle tattle. The other ghosts think he's bringing trouble." Turning and retreating, she began to fade.

"Wait. How did you come in uninvited?"

"This is my home. There will always be a place for me here. A good thing too, since you desperately need my help—as a decorator. Red in the kitchen, really?" She scoffed at the crimson floor tiles and backsplash behind the counter.

"Mom loved that color." Marta blinked, her eyes suddenly too wet.

"No accounting for taste. Either tear out the tiles or paint them white. It looks like a killing room—besides which, red on black is so tacky." She glowed more brightly the more passionately she spoke. "Now, where do you keep your beer? It's been a long thirsty haul getting here."

The next morning, Marta slipped what had been her mother's black blazer over a lace top and straightened her spine in front of the mirror. It didn't erase her teen rebellion and the bitter mother-daughter arguments over clothes, but she made up her face and blow-dried her hair the way Mom preferred.

Soon enough, Marta would go back to school and revert to her usual style, but the hair ritual was an offering to Mom that felt especially appropriate because the solicitor was coming to read the will.

Before breakfast, she went to check on Grandma in the pantry.

The old ghost hovered over the red tiles wearing the same cheap coat, barely visible. She hadn't touched the beer Marta set out the night before. The unopened bottle sat next to an empty glass on the counter. The previous evening, she'd looked solid enough to pass for living, but daylight pierced Grandma's translucent form, fading her to nothing.

"We're meeting in the dining room," Marta said. "Coming?"

"I can't leave the kitchen."

When her brothers built their mansion, they'd kept the original foundation and kitchen walls, so they could get a building permit for a so-called renovation. It saved red tape, cut the wait time, and fended off potential objections by neighbors. Grandma was haunting her old kitchen, part of the old place Grandpa had built when they were squatters living next to the former garbage dump.

"What do you think of the Ashton family compound?" Marta expected congratulations.

Grandma sniffed. "I suppose you could get used to it."

"I expect to inherit my mother's third."

"If you say so..." Grandma faded to outlines in vapor.

"Don't leave. You just got here." Last night, Grandma hadn't felt like chatting. "I have questions about Mom, and this lawyer thing won't take long. Can you wait an hour?"

Grandma turned transparent, her voice more breeze than breath. "Stay out of trouble."

"That's me, Miss Goody Two-Shoes."

"Don't wind up like me—or your mom." What remained of Grandma drifted across the pantry floor and through the wall.

"Wait!" Marta flung open the side door. "What do you mean don't be like Mom?"

Had her mother somehow provoked her killer? Marta stepped into the garden with its trimmed trees and topiary lions, looking up and down the side of the mansion, but the gardens were vacant, right up to the front gate.

21

Waking up exhausted, Tonya forced herself out of bed and padded down the hallway students had abandoned for the holidays. After the usual cacophony of voices and conflicting music, silence creeped her out. She brushed her teeth in the echoey communal bathroom where fluorescent lights tinged her skin green and darkened the circles under her eyes.

Once he finished pacing on the beach, Hatch had kept her awake most of the night with nightmares of flying and falling. Memories flickered of tromping through the bush, but she'd awoken hungry, so at least Hatch hadn't feasted on rodents.

I want my own cave.

And... you're back. I hoped you were giving me the silent treatment. Since Hatch never said anything helpful.

I need a lair to hide my pretties.

While we're chatting, tell me, did you murder Donna Ashton?

Who?

Don't play innocent, Hatch. Short lady, red suits, carries a huge amethyst crystal on a golden scepter.

I didn't kill any human.

Did you break the Staff of Storms?

No, but I'll break your legs if you don't bring me gold.

You can't make me steal.

His chuckle grated like stone against stone. *I already have.*

An hour later, Tonya took the lakeside path out of campus on her way to meet Priya. The plan was to question Ted Kwok. His campground was near the beach where the mayor's body was found. Hatch had denied committing the crime, so Tonya stood straight and squared her shoulders, the previous night's fatigue dropping away. If Hatch was innocent, they didn't belong in jail. All she had to do was prove it.

Let me fly! Hatch bellowed his demands inside her head. *I must hunt.*

His needs for food and treasure overwhelmed her senses. Tonya swooned, grabbed a nearby lamppost, and regained balance. *Shut up and let me think.*

I'm starving for food and treasure. Let me transform or I'll take over.

No. I have to meet Priya. He'd kept her up all night—now he wanted to shift during the day too?

Talk to Priya. Is that all you puny humans ever do?

We're going to find out who killed Donna.

Hatch scoffed. *Time's up. Let's fly.*

Before he could force the change, Tonya argued, *National is going to throw me in a cell and forget about me. You heard Sheriff Anderson explain guilty until proven innocent. How will you fly when they lock me behind bars?*

That shut him up. Tonya hurried west, passing out of the university grounds and not stopping until she reached the wrought iron gate to Loon Lake Cemetery.

She missed strolling through the monuments and reading old headstones. Blackened stumps covered the rolling hills, a grim reminder of her actions, but she felt a twinge of relief to see new saplings thriving beside them. She had organized mass plantings on the island and in the cemetery to atone for starting the fire, but ghosts held eternal grudges. On her latest visit, angry spirits had pelted her with snow.

Sidestepping the cemetery, she walked through the forest that ran alongside it and looked for a stump or stone to sit on while she waited for Priya.

Footsteps sounded on the path behind her.

"Hello?" She glanced over her shoulder.

Hidden by trees, a presence lurked in the shadows. A ghost? She spun around, but the path behind her was empty.

"Show yourself! Whatever you want, face me."

Blushing, Drake stepped out from behind a tree. "I'm sorry if I scared you."

"You're lucky I didn't freak out and use my powers."

"Priya said the police questioned you."

"That was a secret!"

"Not her fault. It came out by accident, and I had to make sure you're okay."

Her pulse raced. She was more than okay. Hatch said he didn't commit the crime, which meant she wasn't a murderer. She could be with Drake!

Absolutely. But if you get your heart's desire, I get mine. Hatch's voice in her head was louder than before. Stronger. *Give me a lair to hide my pretties, and gold and gems to fill it.*

No, she said. *I can't steal for you.*

Then I'll transform you, and while you're blacked out, I'll take my claws and shred Drake to pieces.

No.

Hatch snickered. *Try and stop me.*

She dropped to her knees on the snow.

"What's wrong?" His face clouded with concern; Drake tried to give her a hand.

She pulled her scarf up to hide her tears and got to her feet without touching his hand. The only way to protect her loved ones was to stay away. That or give Hatch what he wanted.

Since the parasite's strength grew alongside his appetites, Tonya couldn't see an end to it. The only safe option was to stay away from anyone she liked that Hatch could threaten. But how could she say goodbye to Drake?

She looked at him. He was obviously concerned but waiting patiently for her to explain. He never pushed her or put his needs ahead of hers. He saw past the college cliques that treated her like an outcast and loved her unconditionally. Tonya would never forget how, on their first date, he told her to ask him anything. Before Hatch, they'd never kept secrets from each other, but he was a Mundane, and the last time she involved him in magical affairs, City Council erased his memories which risked damaging his mind. Never again.

"Admit it." His eyes never left hers. "You're seeing somebody else."

"Where did that come from?"

"We haven't talked properly in months. When I call, you're always busy. Can you remember the last time we went on a date, just the two of us? How about the last time we kissed?"

"Summer." Before Hatch got too strong.

"You've been distant and weird since August." His face flushed. "If you want to break up, this is your chance. I love you, but if you don't love me, then treat me like an adult and tell me."

The start of a headache pulsed in her temples. The situation was completely unfair. How could she be so cruel to Drake?

But the growing dragon had gradually taken control, his demands keeping her too busy to think and his night flights robbing her of sleep and giving her brain fog. With no time to reflect or plan or rest—he'd driven a wedge between Tonya and her friends like some kind of abusive boyfriend.

"Forgive me."

"I want what we used to have."

Intimate friendship, deep kisses, and deeper conversations. He was marriage material, for sure, but how could she string him along when Hatch could take her over? That trick in the jewelry store proved it. Even during the day, Hatch put anyone close to Tonya in danger.

"You're right. This isn't working."

Her voice trembled as the words hit Drake like a slap. The worst part was, if anyone could accept Tonya as a freakish half-woman half-dragon chimera, it was Drake. He'd stood by her side after she sucked the death energy out of Jack Waldock. He'd stuck around Loon Lake after the Ashtons wiped his memories to separate them and returned with greater tenderness when he remembered their budding romance. Loon Lake's conniving Old Families had put Drake and his friends in jeopardy using every weapon from mind control fungus to fireballs, but none of it drove him away.

He loved her after risking their lives together, but this wasn't right. Drake didn't know the danger Tonya put him in.

"I have a magic world secret. Forgive me for avoiding you. I've been distant because I'm hiding from, uh, something worse than a curse." Telling him about Hatch would put him in the crosshairs of the scaley sadist. Hatch could hurt her boyfriend to manipulate her, an activity he would delight in, cruelly and often, until Tonya renounced all control.

Swallowing painfully, she kept her tone even. "I can't have a boyfriend. There is no other guy, but staying together would hurt you. Forgive me?"

"If you're in danger..."

"No."

"You shouldn't be alone."

"Don't."

The look on her face must have clinched it, because his broad shoulders slowly fell and he sighed. "Okay, I'll respect your wishes. But if I go, don't expect me back."

"Good." She clamped her jaw to stop it from trembling.

Standing ramrod straight, Drake marched down the path. She yearned to call after him, to apologize and make up—to kiss him until her pain turned to joy. But to save Drake, the breakup had to be real. Salty tears rolled onto her lips, and she watched his broad shoulders recede until the trees swallowed him up.

22

MARTA, CRAVING A SECOND coffee, followed her brothers into the opulent dining room. The lawyer at the far end of a polished table arranged papers, then quietly tap-tap-tapped his fingers on the computer, the sound echoing in the huge space. Portly and red-faced, he wore a maroon suit with a red tie.

Who dressed this guy, a clown?

Marta took a seat facing her brothers near the midpoint of the table. This left a gap, but she wanted to sit close to the door, so she could slip out if she started to cry. To spare her manicure, she chewed the side of her finger, leg bobbing with energy despite lack of sleep. What did Mom call it? Tired and wired.

She whispered to Marvin, "Grandma spoke to me last night."

"What?" He blanched.

"Told me Dad was coming to this meeting." Marta last saw him when she was nine years old, so why didn't her uncle look surprised?

The roar of a motorcycle coming up the drive unannounced by the guard at the gate answered her question. Marvin was expecting him. Leaving her uncles, she hurried to meet the man who Mom—when she thought Marta couldn't hear—called her "sperm donor."

Something familiar about the Harley Davidson growl comforted her. She recognized his short, powerful build from old snapshots, but not his face.

When Wendel removed the helmet and shook his long graying mane, he revealed a chiseled jaw and manly features in a tanned face etched with fine lines. Like an action hero, he radiated health from the set of his shoulders to his boots vaulting up the steps. No wonder Mom had fallen for him.

Without removing his boots or jacket, Dad burst into the dining room. "Stephen, Marvin!" He thrust out his hand, but her uncles stood aloof. What did they expect after ditching their sister?

Ignoring the snub, he turned to her. "Marta, you look just like your mother!"

She shrugged. After dreaming about this reunion for years, his sudden appearance didn't match her imagination. Despite his handsome face and broad shoulders, his jacket smelled of stale tobacco and zipping it open released a middle-aged paunch cloaked in a faded Iron Maiden shirt.

"I'm not here to cause trouble."

His words reminded Marta of Grandma's warning.

"But Donna's death reminded me you can't predict tomorrow." He held out his hand. "Bygones?"

Dad's imploring expression contradicted the image of a powerful, dangerous man Mom built up over Marta's teen years. Riding a motorcycle didn't make him evil incarnate, but he *was* a terrible father.

Marta wrapped her arms around herself, watching Marvin step forward and shake her father's hand. "Wendel."

"Marvin." Her father turned to Stephen who hesitated, changing emotions scudding across his face like clouds.

Funny. She thought of Marvin as intelligent and sensitive, while Stephen was the spoiled uncle thinking only of himself. Could it be Stephen cared for her feelings after all?

She didn't talk about her father anymore, but her uncles had witnessed her childhood yearnings for a big strong daddy to come home and fix everything.

Faced with this rat-tailed, beer-bellied biker dude, Marta could hardly look at him. What kind of man abandons his wife and kid? He'd never married Mom, but he'd followed Grandpa into the bootleg magic business. Fine, times were tough and they were poor, but his visits home spread further apart until, one day, he'd left them without a goodbye. On nights when Marta cried for her missing daddy, Mom repeated a fairytale. He was working hard for them and would return soon, because he loved her very much.

As if. By age ten, Marta knew they were living on her Mom's receptionist salary. By age eleven, he'd stopped sending her birthday cards.

Did he expect her to greet him with a hug and an I love you? "Why are you here now?" It was obvious Dad had skipped Mom's funeral and timed his arrival for the reading of the will.

"I'm here to see you." His glance wavered to the uncles and back to her. "Your mom and I were common law, sweetie. Her estate goes to me."

Stephen lunged forward and slapped him.

Marta reeled. *He couldn't crash through their grief to steal Mom's money.* She rushed out of the room and stormed out the front door. Resting her hands on her thighs, she watched her breath in the frigid air, the driveway gravel crunching under her dress flats.

Breath slowing, Marta straightened her spine. She was stronger than this. What she needed was strategy and help. She sent a text and waited, wishing for but not expecting a response.

23

It was hard to tell from Marta's text what kind of emergency Tonya was walking into, but the guard waved her through. A first for any member of Tonya's family. Marta had to be desperate.

A uniformed maid answered the door and pointed her toward the opulent dining room Tonya remembered from the wake. The table dwarfed the little family of four. Marvin and Stephen sat together near the center, and the lawyer occupied the far end of the polished surface with a laptop, briefcase, and folders of papers. A weathered dude in faded leathers sporting a thin gray ponytail studied the computer over the lawyer's shoulder, revealing the top of his balding head.

"Sit here," Marta hissed from the near end of the table, bossy as ever.

Why did I come here again?

To find out who killed the mayor, so Anderson won't throw us in a cell and clip my wings, Hatch snapped. *Try to keep up.* He blew out a long sigh that made the inside of Tonya's skull itch.

You are so annoying! But Hatch was right. She'd read enough true crime to know that when a woman is murdered, ninety percent of the time a male relative or partner did it. At Marta's invitation, Tonya could check out the prime suspects while a chubby lawyer dressed in a burgundy suit read them the will. All she had to do was keep her head down, offer Marta emotional support, and find out who lacked an alibi for Monday night.

Marvin spoke to Marta's father in hushed tones with one eye on Stephen like a cook watching a pot. "How was your trip here?"

"Slippery. There's a reason bikers go south for the winter."

"So, you don't plan to stay?" Marta's voice rose in hope.

"I can get a car for the cold months. It would take more than snow to scare me away." He smiled like a snake.

Stephen gripped the arms of his chair, and nobody smiled back.

Marta started some awkward chitchat as if she was trying to get to know this stranger, and Tonya's heart squeezed. When Barbara shunned her, she'd lost her mother and her father in the divorce. But Marta's loss was greater. After growing up without a father, somebody had murdered her mother.

Tonya made a silent vow to find out who killed Donna Ashton, even if the truth implicated Hatch. Marta deserved closure.

Stephen glowered at the man who had abandoned his sister.

The lawyer tapped his laptop screen with a pen. "We should start."

The uncles and Marta resumed their seats.

Marta's dad dragged a chair beside the lawyer and craned his neck to read the screen over his shoulder.

"Wendel." The lawyer cleared his throat a few times, but the guy didn't take the hint.

Ignoring him, the lawyer pulled a thin stack of papers out of his briefcase. The preamble was long and full of legal terms. Tonya watched Marta's eyelids droop until he said, "Donna willed her personal belongings to her daughter."

"What about the Boathouse and Ashton Security?" Wendel asked.

"The Boathouse is owned jointly by all the Mods, but the security business belongs to the family."

Marta's father stood, the muscles of his tree-trunk legs bulging through tight black leather. "In other words, it's mine. My money built it, so I own the house and land." He glared at Stephen. "I financed the security business from day one. It belongs to me too."

"You want to contest Ms. Ashton's will?" The lawyer's expression and voice remained bland.

"What will? Donna and I were common law married. I should get her property, not her brothers. Who asked for your opinion anyway?"

"I did." Marvin remained in his seat, arms crossed, twin pencils poking out of his shirt pocket. "And I paid him to track you down out of courtesy."

"You mean to see if I was dead."

Stephen whined, "Where've you been for ten years?"

"You're done here." Wendel towered over the lawyer. "Get out and don't send me the bill!"

The lawyer continued, his voice slow and calm. "Ashton Security and this property are not owned by individuals. The company controls all assets, and Donna Ashton lost her interest in Ashton Security when she died."

"I'm owed my inheritance!" Wendel paced, turned, looked at his fists and paced again, as if his body couldn't contain the emotion turning his face red.

"It's explained in here." The lawyer offered a thick envelope of papers. "The articles of incorporation are very clear. This is a private family business linked to the Ashton name. Ownership of the family compound, Ashton Security, the wall, and the jail are held equally by the surviving siblings until they die, at which point Marta Ashton will inherit. If Donna's brothers have surviving children, Marta will share her inheritance equally with them."

"This isn't over!" Wendel yelled at the lawyer. "I'll sue you!"

When he left, Marvin cracked open a window to dissipate the odor of sweaty leather and stale smoke.

What a relief.

He smelled okay, Hatch objected. *What's better than smoke?*

Tonya ignored him. Finally, some clues. She watched rainbows dance on the crystal chandeliers, waiting for the maid to bring coffee and sweets. The family had to be multimillionaires.

The contract eliminated Marta's father as a murder suspect and spelled out how much Marvin and Stephen stood to gain from eliminating their sister.

Subtly, she texted Marta.

Find out where your uncles were on Monday night.

Always discrete, Marta pointed at Stephen. "Where were you Monday night?"

"Stuck in Loon Lake Village," Stephen whined. "There's nowhere to park anymore and nowhere to walk with the cruise ships. Stupid tourists crowded me out of my favorite bar."

"City Council is useless," Marvin added. "We struggled to keep the peace before Donna died, but now it's worse. Yesterday a witch spelled a hole in her jail cell and escaped. She could have been a murderer, but when I told that new Sheriff Anderson, he said National didn't meddle in small stuff." Marvin sighed. "What are we supposed to do with rowdy practitioners if our cells can't hold them?"

"You could run for mayor and change the law," said Stephen.

Marvin rounded on him. "Haven't I done enough?"

"Sorry," Stephen mumbled.

The grovel seemed out of character, but how well did Tonya know any of these people beyond their public personas?

"Where were you on Monday?" Tonya asked Marvin.

He reacted as if a dog had suddenly spoken. Marvin stepped to Tonya but failed to intimidate her, because she was tall enough to look him in the eye. "I was with Stephen, not that it's your business." He asked Marta, "What's she doing here?"

Tonya answered for her. "Emotional support person. Marta wasn't looking forward to meeting Wendel alone."

"What's that supposed to mean?" Stephen did tower over Tonya, and his facial muscles flexed in unpleasant ways.

"Are you good, Marta?" Tonya asked.

When she nodded, Tonya waved goodbye and showed herself out, her mind sifting through clues and possibilities. The beach where Donna had been found wasn't far from Loon Lake Village. Could the Mayor have got into a dispute with an angry tourist? Somebody must have seen something, and if they had, National would know.

She pulled out her phone and dialed Inspector Anderson.

"Tonya, you found a witness to confirm your alibi!" He sounded upbeat, probably sure of her innocence.

"I can't confirm it, so I'm working on Option B."

That comment earned Tonya some dead air, but she didn't feel like explaining. "Have you talked to people in Loon Lake Village? The mayor might have been there trying to settle a dispute."

"Yes, we canvassed thoroughly, and no, she wasn't seen in The Village on Monday."

"The Village." She whistled. "You sound like a local."

"Thanks. Helen's been coaching me, and she loaned me a colony of charmed rabbits to watch the perimeter of Loon Lake City. Nobody gets in or out of the Village or downtown without us knowing."

"Including tourists?"

"First thing we did was block the ship from teleporting. It can't leave until I find the murderer."

"The tourists must be delighted."

That comment earned a chuckle, which gave Tonya the confidence to press on. "Marta let me sit in on the reading of the will, and I have a question. Are the Ashtons having money trouble?"

"I don't like Option B. You're a civilian. Worry about your alibi and let me investigate crime. Local police are proving very cooperative."

"They are?"

"Well, they won't remember it afterward, but officers are going door-to-door looking for witnesses who saw the event. Or you. Out of loyalty to Helen, I'm trying to corroborate your alibi for you."

Oh great. "Thanks."

After they hung up, Tonya went with her instincts. If the Ashtons were in financial trouble, there'd be gossip. With ghosts passing through walls and observing friends and foes alike, it was hard to keep a juicy secret. She assumed the Ashton brothers had no money motive.

Pondering her next move, Tonya heard someone fall into step behind her. Thinking Anderson or one of his police helpers might be tailing her, she spun to face her pursuer, not expecting to see Roberto. The uppity Adonis had courted

Priya to use her powers then dropped her once he'd gotten what he wanted. It would delight Tonya to discover he was the murderer.

"Shouldn't you be on the island taming a dragon or something?"

"Sure, but first you need to speak to my mother."

24

CROSSING LOON LAKE IN an aluminum boat, Grace shivered as glacial air cut through her coat and jeans. The lake was choppy, kicking spray into her face. She clapped her gloved hands to force blood into her fingertips. Why had she suggested this? A winter film shoot had sounded like a much better idea from the warmth of the Hub Pub, and when she made it a challenge, Zain had to accept immediately.

Their fifteen-foot boat took ages to chug past the cruise ship, its glow faintly visible by daylight. Reaching open water, Zain opened the throttle on the outboard motor.

"Hold on to your bagels." Their little craft climbed the whitecaps and thudded into the troughs.

Grace gripped the thin vinyl cushion on the bench which scarcely softened the impact. Her fingers ached, and her toes were going to drop off before they reached the island. With frostbitten fingers, she'd never hold the camera steady. She got up and held Zain around the waist for stability, yelling close to his ear, "It's not too late to back out! I promise not to mock your loser butt in front of the Ninjas."

"Ha!" He lifted his hands from the wheel to rub them together. "Nice try. I'm already tasting the sweet, sweet ice cream of victory. Be prepared to grovel in defeat."

The contest was simple. Each would take turns operating the camera so they could shoot scenes from an improvised horror movie. The Digital Ninjas would watch the rushes and decide whose footage would make the cut into their latest masterpiece "Death on Ice."

There was no script which gave Grace the edge as a trained actor, but Zain had wild ideas and loved to subvert cheesy horror tropes. She anticipated a close contest, especially since Zain had set the rules.

One: They had to film in and around Betty's abandoned shack on the island.

Two: It had to be a Christmas horror movie.

Three: The Digital Ninjas would vote on clips of two to ten minutes for inclusion in the finished movie. The filmmaker with the most clips chosen would win.

Grace had insisted on the time limit, otherwise Zain would shoot a feature film. When his eyes lit up like that, he wouldn't feel hunger, cold, or fatigue until he reached his goal. Not so for Grace. Before the contest started, riding to the island made her teeth chatter all the way to the dock.

"Beware Dragon" warned a large sign beside the public pier.

"Is that for real?" Grace asked.

"The dragon lives in a cave under this island." Zain's shoulders hunched as he peered overhead. "Tonya says it works for Ashton Security."

"Great," Grace said sarcastically. "So don't rob any banks and it won't roast us alive."

She watched the sky on the short walk to Betty's shack on the beach. The Recluse of Loon Lake had never actually lived there. It was a decoy for the magically camouflaged home on the hill above it. According to Tonya, magic bootleggers built the shack in the 1940s.

Were their ghosts still haunting the premises? Since Priya had explained they existed, and that she could see them all over Loon Lake, Grace never felt 100% safe. Sneaky spirits could be watching them right now, laughing at their foolish confidence and waiting for sundown to attack.

"Do you think there will be ghosts in the shack?" A year ago, that question would have sounded foolish coming out of her mouth, but Grace had seen a lot of strange things in Loon Lake.

"Ghosts aren't supposed to appear on the island," Zain said. "Magic doesn't work either."

Grace pointed to the hill over the shack. "Then how come Betty's home is still hidden?"

"I dunno." As Zain trudged to the shack, weighed down by cameras and equipment, Zain pointed skyward at a silvery dragon with a rainbow sheen. "What a beauty!"

Grace stifled a scream. The dragon swooped so close, she could count the plates on its belly.

"She will be my star!" Zain dropped everything but the camera around his neck and chased after the dragon.

Muttering to herself, Grace picked up the extra equipment and hauled it in front of the shack. The back of her neck prickled, and she didn't want to enter alone, but she needed to stand close to shelter in case the dragon returned. Flores had attacked Tonya and Zain in the summer, and what if Roberto couldn't call off his hungry dragon?

Out of breath, Zain returned, knees dusty and shirt dirty.

Grace took him tenderly by the shoulders gazing into his eyes. "What's wrong?"

"Nothing."

"Did the dragon hurt you?"

Zain forced a laugh that ended in a wheeze. "She'd have to catch me first." He threw open the door of the shack and strode in.

Grace followed but damp odors assaulted her nose. Tufts of stuffing puffed out of a vintage sofa, the perfect cradle for vermin. "Let's work outside. This place smells like mice."

"But the price was nice. Help me dress the set." He tacked a row of Christmas stockings to the window ledge. "There's a full moon tonight. It's going to be perfect."

"Which is why I'm going to beat you."

Grace didn't love slasher flicks, but she knew how to captivate a viewer. At least, that's what Zain had been telling her since he recruited her for his last horror film. Thick black hair that stuck out in all directions partially hid the side of his face, and she recognized the glint in his eye. Film was his passion. He would come out to shoot in frigid temperatures, competition or no competition, which would make it all the sweeter when she beat him at his own game.

Zain couldn't help bragging about his ideas. "I'm making this crazy movie about a were-reindeer that transforms into a killer elf when the moon is full."

"So, it's a comedy?"

"What makes you say that?" he asked with a straight face.

The Ninjas wouldn't vote for anything with bad special effects. All she had to do to beat Zain was to film how vulnerable she felt in this terrible place. With the camera on a tripod, her authentic shivering and fear of ghosts would come through and win the day. The secret was making the viewer feel something. Jump scares and gimmicks were for amateurs. She could create suspense using nothing but good acting and mood lighting. Zain was going down.

"Ladies first." Zain checked the camera around his neck. "Where do you want me?"

"Oh, no you don't. I want to film my part after dark. You go first."

"Fine but promise not to laugh at my costume."

When he came out of the shack ten minutes later, damn but Zain looked hot in green shorts and a Santa hat. Grace didn't whistle, but her glance must have lingered too long. Zain grinned, his kissable mouth full of vicious monster teeth. What a shock! She hated to admit it, but maybe Zain was on to something with this killer elf idea.

They took turns shooting "day for night" and at dusk, and by full dark they'd recorded their bits and put away the equipment. Loaded with packs, they trudged along the beach but stopped before reaching the pier.

A mountainous creature sat on the shore, blocking access to their boat. Its eyes glowed dull gold as it unfurled bat-like wings in silhouette against the moon.

Grace backed away slowly, but Zain hurried forward. "Here, little dragon. Here Flores." He reached his hand back to Grace and whispered, "Give me the camera before we scare it away."

She fumbled in her pack while she retreated. The monster tensed its legs to leap into the air, not at Zain, so she crept behind Zain and gave him the camera.

In one bound, the beast jumped into the sky, climbing until it shrank to a bat-sized silhouette against the moon. Zain filmed the whole thing until the beast shrank out of sight. Then he trained his camera light on the shack. He played the light up and down until she had to ask, "What do you see?"

"Something." He walked to a pile of fallen leaves and pushed them around with his feet.

Long white sticks protruded from the pile. To Grace they looked like branches from paper birch trees. "What's so great about a pile of leaves?"

Zain used his DSLR to shoot the leaves from all angles. "We can run the closing credits over this. It's perfect."

Grace tried to see what Zain was talking about. On closer inspection, the white branches resolved into bones. "Do you think a bear died here?"

"Or a moose." Zain kicked away more leaves, revealing scattered leg bones.

Grace used her hands to clear away more leaves until a spine and ribs stood out distinctly in the moonlight. She tried not to imagine scavengers cleaning the bones to make them white. In the wintry air, the skeleton still smelled faintly of rotten meat.

"Too bad for you I saw it first." Zain cackled. "This is going to kill!"

25

THE LAST THING TONYA remembered was Roberto's sad smile.

A draft chilled her face, and she pushed against cold sand to sit up. Overhead, lightbulbs swung on cords revealing an enormous space demarcated by canvas and tent poles. The red pavilion?

No. This was an actual tent made of canvas on the inside. They were on the island where Roberto lived with Flores. He'd knocked her out and taken her to the island. She jumped to her feet and tried to leave but manacles cut into her ankles, chained to an upright support post.

"Help! Let me go!" She thrashed and kicked, trying to break free, but the restraints bruised her ankles. She shouted louder. "Help! Help!"

A low rumbling grew behind her and warmed her back in the frigid air. *It was about time they put on the heat.*

But the temperature increased, and with it the stench of rotten meat.

She turned to find the source of the heat and found herself staring into a giant mouth full of yellow teeth. She dived –

—Just in time to avoid a fiery dragon blast. It was Flores, her white, rainbow scales muted in the low lighting. Her teeth much, much too close.

"Please." Tonya held up her hands. "I'm not here to fight. Let me go?"

The dragon launched itself at Tonya who deked to the side, but leg irons yanked her back to land on her face, arms spread in front of her. She braced herself for the end, instant cremation, her hands covering the back of her head as if they could fend off dragon breath.

"Bad Flores. Sit!"

Tonya peeked over her shoulder. Roberto had a silver whistle in his mouth and a burlap bag that squirmed in one hand. When Flores sat up like a dog begging for treats, Roberto walked closer and stretched out his hand. The dragon lowered its head and allowed him to pet the side of its scaley visage and scratch it under the chin. When he stepped back, the dragon watched every move, tail up and quivering, as Robert grabbed a rat out of the bag and threw it. Flores snapped it out of the air and nodded at Roberto, letting out a rumble of contentment.

Tonya had seen enough. "Let me go now! Your dragon tried to kill me."

Roberto's smile faded. "Relax. I won't let Flores hurt you."

"She could eat you in one gulp. What can you do against a dragon?"

"She loves me." He looked up at Flores. "Don't you, *Flor de ma vida*?"

"Let me out of these irons. She likes you, but she hates me." Tonya had killed her mate.

"If I take them off, will you run?"

"No," Tonya lied. "I'm curious. Why did you bring me here?"

"Mami needs to speak to you." He moved in closer to whisper. "She wants to know how you turn into a dragon, so tell her and make it interesting. If your explanations bore her..." He avoided her eyes with a guilty look. "It's fine, just don't be boring."

Now Tonya really had to get out of there. Paloma Alvarez sounded more temperamental than the dragon, and if Flores recognized Tonya as the one who killed her mate and sought revenge, Roberto wouldn't be able to calm her with a bag of rodent treats.

"My ankles really hurt. Any chance I could wait for her in a chair?" Tonya looked at Flores. "I'm too small to fight you, and if you needed backup, you do have a dragon."

"Let me go brush my teeth first," he said. "I'll bring you a cup of tea."

Tonya looked at Flores, who lay in downward dog position, her head resting on her front claws, eyes closed. Her professor would not approve, and this could get out of hand, but what choice did Tonya have? She closed her eyes, opened herself to life force, and fell back, blown to her feet by the dragon's twenty-megaton glow.

She had killed its mate to stop a murderous rampage, and in self-defense she was going to kill Flores. With regret, Tonya began to draw out the dragon's life force.

Flores leaped, bellowing and blasting random breaths of fire. Overhead, the tent started burning as lights and tent poles fell. Roberto rushed in and fought the flames with a fire extinguisher.

The commotion broke Tonya's concentration, but she focused on the dragon again, drawing delicious life force into herself.

No! Hatch screamed in Tonya's head and shut down her powers. *Try that again and I'll kill every one of your friends and your family barbecue style!*

26

A PUFF OF VAPOR appeared, white against the dark smoke from the fire. Sheriff Anderson stepped out. With a deliberate flick of the fingers, he magicked her leg irons open and pulled her toward him.

Over the dragon's bellows and the whoosh of flames, he yelled, "Tonya Jones, I'm arresting you for attacking this dragon, property of the Alvarez family."

She struggled against his rock-hard arms. "They kidnapped me! I had to escape."

In her ear, he said, "Don't make me add resisting arrest and arson to the charges."

He marched her into the cloud, followed by Paloma. A moment later, the three of them stepped out into a waiting room with colorful murals of a beach and a volcano. Plastic building blocks littered the floor and upbeat Muzak played in the background.

"Why is she here?" Tonya asked.

"Cooperate, or I will have to sedate you." Paloma flashed a huge needle.

Anderson walked them past the vacant reception desk and into a corridor lined with examination rooms. At the end of the hall, they entered a large room where a vampire lay handcuffed to a hospital bed connected to a blood red IV bag.

"Kidnapping is against the law." Breathlessly, Tonya made her case to Anderson. "You should arrest her. I had to escape, because her dragon threatened to kill me." *Tell him, Hatch.*

"Calm yourself. Sit." Senora Alvarez patted a gurney. "I need to give you a simple examination to make sure you're fit to stand trial."

"I'm not guilty." Although maybe Hatch was. "You can't hijack innocent people and put them in leg irons."

"You, innocent?" Paloma's smile deepened the wrinkles around her mouth. "There's blood on your claws. I can almost smell it." Her expression softened to one of concern. "Why didn't you come to me for help when I offered, before it was too late?"

"Like you took care of Priya? Using Roberto to tap her powers and turn baby dragons into fire-breathers?"

If this was news to Anderson, he showed no surprise.

"Settle down, dear. This will be over soon."

Paloma brandished her needle and Tonya tried to hop off the gurney, but Anderson held her in place, his arms too strong to budge. There was nothing she could do. Tonya stopped fighting and screamed.

It burned going in, and shortly after, turned her limbs to straw. Everything went black as she collapsed onto the thin mattress.

Was she out for a minute? An hour? She stared into a super bright light like dentists use. A cluster of doctors and nurses in surgical scrubs stared down at her. Paloma stood off to one side, lecturing them, but Tonya couldn't concentrate. Her eyelids drooped and her thoughts kept wandering into dreams. Paloma's Peruvian accent reminded her of Roberto which reminded her of Priya which reminded her of sculptures which reminded her of lightning. Trapped in a nightmare, she tried to get up.

Thick straps immobilized her arms and legs, and when she opened her mouth to scream, nothing came out. She couldn't run, like in a paralysis dream where monsters are coming but you can't escape.

Except in this scenario, Tonya was awake, and the monsters were real.

27

Tonya struggled to consciousness, roused by the sound of her name. Bright lights dazzled her eyes, and she wore a hospital gown. *Where were her clothes?*

"I'm breaking you out of here." Sheriff Anderson stood beside her hospital bed and gently slid the IV needle out of her arm. "Can you stand?"

Thick straps held her down. He released her wrists and ankles, but her heavy limbs resisted movement. "My head's spinning." Nothing felt quite real.

"They'll come back soon. May I?"

He slung her arm over his meaty shoulder and took her hand in a firm grasp, helping her to her feet. When she couldn't stand, he put her over his shoulder and raced through a narrow corridor, down a fire escape, and set her down on a floor Tonya didn't remember. They must have moved her while she slept.

Eventually, they reached a shadowy room where even Tonya's dragon senses strained to see his face. Shadows moved in the dark, coming in and out of focus like black-on-black ghosts.

Is this your new boyfriend? Hatch cackled. *Let's show him what you can do!*

Anderson froze. He circled Tonya, inhaling. "You smell like a dragon shifter, but you weren't lying. There really is another entity living inside you."

"And he's a total jerk."

See what I have to put up with?

Anderson offered Tonya a hand and pulled her through a door, which tickled. Very strange.

They emerged into a starry night and enjoyed a breath of freedom. Except she couldn't recognize one landmark—not one monument, street, or familiar barn to situate them in Loon Lake.

"Where are we?"

"Can you walk?"

She nodded. How had she never noticed how handsome he was?

"Good. I want you to see my parents' country."

Miles of pink and purple foothills stretched between them and a conical peak. "Your parents live beside a mountain?"

"Don't be silly. They live inside."

He started up a stony path overgrown with ferns and hung with flowering vines. By the halfway point the air was hot and dry, and there was no more vegetation on the path. Amethyst sparkled in crevices, and crystal stalactites dangled at the edge of little caves. The muggy air smelled like burning cotton candy. The higher they got, the more it felt like walking into a furnace.

"I'll pass out from the heat before we reach the top. Please, take me home."

"Relax," he said. "We're not walking."

"Really? Where'd you hide the helicopter, in your pocket?"

Stupid human.

That was a joke, she told Hatch.

I'll show you who's in charge! He started to make her shift.

No, Hatch. Stop! The detective mustn't see her lose control.

But Sheriff Anderson was doubled over. Strain etched lines across his face, and his bones cracked with snaps and crunch sounds. The flesh flowed under his skin, which stretched as his body expanded. He turned red and scales erupted all over him. As he doubled and tripled in size, his clothing fell in tatters to the stoney ground.

In minutes, she would be alone on a mountain with a hungry dragon.

Hatch! I change my mind.

Puny human, I have decided to honor your request, Hatch practically purred. *No changing in front of Anderson.*

She backed away until she was on the edge of the cliff in rocky terrain that offered no hiding places. Behind Anderson, she spotted a crevice. If she could skirt around him while he was transforming, maybe she could hide in there.

She sidled away from the expanding dragon until she felt air under her heels. Any farther and she'd fall off the cliff. When she took a big step sideways, the dragon's head turned, tracking her with his eyes. When she shuffled in the opposite direction, he opened his mouth.

"No!"

Flames roiled in his throat, rising through his mouth. He'd broil her alive if she didn't jump.

But as quickly as it started, the dragon's outer expansion stopped and he shrank, reversing the process so that red scales faded to human flesh and leathery wings reabsorbed into a fit body that turned to face away at the crucial moment. Tonya got a glimpse of powerful legs before he slipped into a pair of undies and a torn shirt.

"I thought your dragon was going to eat me." Tonya tiptoed farther down the path which shimmered like a mirage.

He gestured to the horizon. "Welcome to my dream world."

"It's incredible." Hills in the distance rose smooth and colorful as modeling clay. "Is that a volcano?" Tonya pointed to a red smoking mountain near the horizon.

"You're observant."

And idiotic.

"How do we get back to Loon Lake?"

His expression softened. "First, let me teach you to fly."

She shuddered.

"I won't hurt you. I'm here to help. Why do you think I became a cop?"

"Good benefits, excellent pension, early retirement?"

"Snark. Good. That sounds like something a dragon would say. Consider this a private interview away from the prying eyes of National."

"We already had an interview, and time to prove my alibi."

"Until somebody reported an unknown dragon breathing fire over a farmer's field."

Hatch!

Anderson wagged a finger. "You call yourself Hatch when you're a dragon?"

"I'm never a dragon. Hatch is when he takes over."

She's not lying, dragon man.

Anderson's eyes widened. Obviously, he could hear Hatch, but a sudden ringing in her head prevented her from listening to the telepathic argument that ensued. In response to Hatch's telepathic ranting, Anderson nodded, paced, and gestured, but she couldn't hear anything clearly until he said, "You're an ordinary human but also a dragon?"

"I'm a witch, you know, Helen's daughter." Describing her powers would complicate matters when what she needed was to return home. Had he taken her into another dimension? She appreciated the pretty scenery and precious minerals, but the air didn't smell natural.

"A witch who's a dragon. I need to see this to believe it. Go on. Change."

"Hatch transforms me against my will. It's never my choice."

Don't listen to the tricky human. Obviously, she is lying.

"If I wake up when Hatch has transformed, he flies extra high to spite me. I'm afraid of heights, and he gets his kicks terrorizing me."

No, I don't.

"He sometimes does barrel rolls until I black out."

Anderson stroked his chin. "If you're afraid of heights, why don't you land?"

"When Hatch takes over, I have no control. Please help get him out of me!"

"You need to learn how to shift when you want." His brow furrowed. "We should stay here and practice until you can do it."

"Not here. Please take me home." She wanted to get out of this place. Everything about it looked and felt wrong. The burning cotton candy smell turned to sulfur.

"Watch me shift. Think about becoming a dragon," he said. "You'll want to join me, and the shift will come naturally."

"Will it always hurt?"

"Yeah, shifting hurts, but it gets easier." Without appearing to strain, he shifted.

She craned her neck up to take in the incredible sight of a red dragon with a golden sheen on its scales. His muscular form was twice as big as he'd become the first time and unmistakably male. He roared and dipped his long neck to look her in the eyes. Brimstone breath ruffled her hair and tickled her nose. She froze, in case movement triggered his predatory instincts. What a magnificent creature, swaggering in its dominance.

His dominance.

Show-off. How wonderful it would be to start the change at will. Inside, part of her yearned to join him. This was it. The instinct that would trigger the change. Eyes closed, she concentrated on becoming Hatch.

No change ...

Hatch laughed. *Nice try trying to become me, but how's that gonna work when you hate me?*

Visualization and wishful thinking weren't working. A whiff of Anderson's dragon pheromones made her heart race, but that didn't trigger the transformation either.

The worst part was disappointing the sheriff. He might lose his job for sneaking her out of National. *Please, Hatch, turn us into a dragon so we can go home.*

Nope. It's too much fun watching you struggle. Besides, whenever I ask for gold you refuse.

"Sorry, I give up." She stood, arms crossed, surveying the twinkling stars in a midnight blue sky, a vision which clashed with the smooth, colorful mountains. *Where was this place?*

With a roar, the red dragon circled around from behind. Her bare feet lifted, and she was airborne, dangling from his claws.

"Put me down!" She screamed but didn't wriggle in case he dropped her on the rocks.

With powerful strokes, he flew her up the mountain where smoke rose from the opening of an active volcano. As they approached, the hazy air turned sulfurous. Sweat trickled between her shoulder blades.

Anderson's scales protected him against the heat, and his family might live happily inside a volcano, but if the air got any hotter, it was going to melt her lungs.

They wound their way up and around the volcano until Tonya's head spun.

I'm going to set you down on that ledge. Listen with an open mind and try what I ask.

"Okay." She was dangling from a dragon's claws. What else could she say?

The ledge was so narrow that the enormous red dragon could barely stand on it, and the clay-like ground sank beneath his feet, leaving a path of footprints all the way to a nearby cave. When he went inside, Tonya watched the play of shadows on the walls as his massive body shrank and reformed.

The sheriff reemerged wearing a coverall and dusting cobwebs off his bare shoulders. "Put these on." He gave her denim coveralls and a yellow helmet with a lamp on the front.

"What's the helmet for?"

"You'll get dirty, and if you stand up straight, you'll crack your head on the ceiling."

"I can crouch."

"Trust me, you want to wear it."

The helmet smelled, but she put on the equipment and followed him into the cave.

Ten minutes later, she crouched in a narrow passage as the detective illuminated their way with a headlamp. The damp walls grew yellow mold, and the air was hot and humid. Anderson was *completely* wrong about the helmet. She'd *only* stood up absentmindedly *three times* cracking her head on the roof.

Was that sarcasm? Hatch asked. *Congratulations, you're more like me every day.*

Shut up, Hatch. You're a guest in this body. Show some respect.

Like you respect me?

Paying no attention to their telepathic squabbles, the sheriff forged ahead. Tonya crept after him, wishing she had a water bottle. Anderson stopped when they reached a metal vault. He punched a code into a keypad and turned a flywheel until it clicked open. On a carved ebony table covered in gold leaf, a strongbox overflowed with treasure.

"Gems. Gold!" Her heart raced, and she thrust her hands into the box, scooping up handfuls of heavy gold coins and letting them flow through her hands.

"We'll make a dragon of you yet."

"Hatch wants me to eat the gold."

"In human form, you can't." He lifted a thermos out of the box. "I've got what we need. Let's build a fire and get to work."

They backtracked to the mouth of the cave where he located cords of neatly stacked firewood. Anderson leaned five logs against each other like a teepee.

The terrain was bare and dry. Tonya said, "I don't see any kindling."

"No need." He opened his lips wide and blew a plume of flame at the wood. The campfire crackled merrily.

"How did you do that?"

"It's a shifter trick. I let my mouth and insides partially change. Don't you try it."

"I'd be happy if I could stay conscious when Hatch takes over."

"That's why we're here. Drink this."

Anderson offered a thermos of bitter liquid that felt cold on her lips but heated her stomach. Sweat beaded on her upper lip and she rubbed her arms, unable to get comfortable.

"I'm burning inside."

"Good. This is what we give young dragons with shifting problems."

"I'm not a shifter, and it's making my stomach too hot." She stood quickly, bonking her helmet on the cave roof. "Are you sure it won't hurt me?"

"The potion is safe." He put his big hand on her shoulder, and his deep voice calmed her. "It revs up the fire-making organs."

"What if I don't have any?" Sweat dripped from every pore, and she was suddenly self-conscious. *Did her armpits smell? Would a dragon man care?* There was no time to ponder as her feet doubled in size, knocking her off balance while her face expanded and her eyeballs bulged like an old-school cartoon. *What was happening?*

The weirder it felt, the more closely she listened to his advice.

"Take a deep breath. Hold it. Exhale slowly."

He led Tonya through a series of visualizations in which Tonya imagined herself transformed and flying without fear. It was pleasant to bask in his attention listening to his deep voice, but her body refused to turn dragon.

This is pointless, and it's making me hungry. Hatch whined and ranted that he didn't appreciate Tonya trying to claim his power.

She ignored Hatch, but his nagging triggered a headache and prevented her from visualizing, so she called a timeout. Anderson sat beside her in silence watching the red coals fade.

"I'm sorry."

"Don't apologize." His eyes were the same green in dragon and human form. "People fear pain, heights, loss of control. To fly you must overcome your fears."

"Meditation can't teach me to fly, because I'm not a real dragon. Hatch forces me to shift whenever he wants, and it's ruining my life. If it wasn't for Hatch, I'd have a boyfriend who understands me, a group of friends I'm not putting in danger, and classes to control my magic so I can safely move away from Loon Lake. Instead, Paloma wants me as her Guinea pig, I'm facing murder charges, and I can't remember what happened Monday night because Hatch was in control."

"That's the real reason I'm here, isn't it?" she asked. "You think if you gain my trust, I'll confess. Well, here's my confession. I don't know who killed Donna

Ashton, but I was trying to figure it out when Paloma captured me and you arrested me. Please, tell me there's a cure."

"Cure?" The sheriff narrowed his eyes. "Do you mean a way to kill Hatch?"

"Hatch is a sadistic parasite, and I want him out of me. Who in their right mind would put up with his abuse?"

I have the same right to live as you.

"He's right. When you talk about getting rid of Hatch, I suspect you *are* capable of murder."

"Hatch is a bloodthirsty psychopath who tortures me by eating furry animals."

Suck it up.

Anderson helped her up from the log. "There's one more thing to try."

"Don't push me off the cliff."

"Of course not. Trust me?"

She didn't really, but in a tiny voice she said, "Yes."

"Could you repeat that?"

"Yes."

The shift started, his body expanding, stretching, changing color and growing scales, claws, a tail, but this time it was over in seconds.

Wow.

"Surprising me won't help. I don't have the hiccups." Before Tonya could elaborate, the dragon cradled her in his arms, carried her out of the cave, and leaped off the cliff.

Her stomach dropped as he flapped his wings, but she stayed quiet as they rose through patches of candy floss clouds in a light blue sky. The tropical sun was rising, and this time there was no fear he might drop her. Anderson did the same thing with shifter kids, he'd said. She wasn't his first learn-to-fly project.

As he clutched her against his chest, his hot scales warmed her, and his thundering heartbeat sent vibrations through her entire body.

As she relaxed, Hatch chimed in, *Time to do a barrel roll, Anderson. Let's go!*

Ignoring Hatch, the dragon flew toward the glinting edge of a sea beyond the mountains. During the entire flight, Tonya never once felt nauseous or faint. They descended to a beach with golden sand where he set her lightly on her feet.

"Hatch complains that you aren't good in the air and you always want to go swimming. I thought you could try transforming in your favorite element. No more fire potions. No more air. Maybe you're a water dragon."

They stood on the edge of the lake, the far shore disappearing in a distant haze. It was warm despite being far from the colorful volcano and a million miles from Loon Lake. The piercing sun and sparkling aqua water felt like the Caribbean.

"Where are we?"

"It's best not to question where we are."

"I don't see anyone around." The sky darkened when Tonya stared at it too long, and the sparkling water grew murky with shadows. "And the landscape is reacting to me."

"We should leave before nightfall."

It was hard to remember whether it was morning or afternoon in this timeless place. She shivered and removed her shoes at the waterline, letting tiny waves roll over her toes. The ocean was soothing but not cold. Brine and seaweed perfumed the air, and the water called to her, stronger than the usual desire to swim on a sweltering day. She whipped off her coverall and waded in. When the gentle waves reached waist level, she lifted off the hospital gown.

On shore, she noticed the sheriff had turned away.

She made a ball of her clothes and launched them onshore. In her bra and panties, Tonya swam for deeper water, her powerful front crawl eating up the distance until the water turned cold and she couldn't see the bottom.

No, you don't. You can't force me to shift by giving yourself hypothermia.

Tonya floated on her back, watching pink puffy clouds scud against the dazzling blue sky. *Shift me into dragon form, so the sheriff is satisfied and we can go home.*

Not a chance, feeble human. He made a deal with me, so you're on your own.

Tonya treaded water and shouted to the detective on shore. "You made a deal with Hatch?"

"Is that what he says?" Anderson shrugged. "He's a liar and possibly much worse. Control Hatch and control yourself. Until you can do that, it isn't safe for you to roam free."

"He refuses to let me control shifting and wants me to give my body to him."

"If you can't figure out how to stay conscious and in control, you could shift by accident and kill someone. Under National's jurisdiction, that's the death penalty."

He's bluffing, Hatch whispered in Tonya's head.

I'm not, the sheriff answered.

For the first time, Tonya and Hatch wanted the same thing—freedom. She dove into the waves and tried to bring on the change but, for whatever reason, Hatch still refused to help. She held her breath and shivered for nothing, skin stinging from the cold. Dive after dive she tried to start the process, but it was futile. Defeated, she waded out of the water, shivering and wishing she had a towel. Instead, she slipped her body into the hospital gown and sat on a fallen palm to dry.

The sheriff was bare chested but wearing the coverall from the waist down. He lifted a flask out of his backpack.

"No more disgusting potions." She wrinkled her nose.

He handed her the flask and strode into the water. "Trust me, you'll feel a lot warmer."

The last time hadn't been too bad, and she was shivering. "Whatever doesn't kill you ..." She toasted Anderson's receding body with the flask and downed the potion, wincing at its bitterness.

A furnace raged inside, heating her and drying her hair as well. Full of energy, Tonya rushed back into the waves and sprinted to catch Anderson.

Few people swam as fast as she did, so it surprised her that Anderson had to stop and wait for her to catch up. Their efficient front crawl strokes matched perfectly, although his larger muscles gave him an advantage. They paced each other for a while, then they treaded water, chatting and rolling onto their backs to exhale like whales. In response, the surrounding water took on pink and purple hues, glittering with golden lights. *Was that a pink dolphin swimming by?*

To show off, Tonya did some breaststroke, backstroke, and butterfly. Not to be outdone, Anderson executed a perfect fly stroke as they raced for the rainbow-hued horizon. Tonya paced him until she was out of breath.

Anderson pulled ahead, revealing a tail swishing in the water to give him extra propulsion. He'd done a partial shift.

"Cheater!" Heat from her belly radiated through her limbs as her temper exploded, triggering movement, swelling, expansion ... this was it! Bones migrated, wings and claws grew, and a tail sprouted from her backbone, long and sinuous.

Pain paralyzed her.

She couldn't breathe.

Her heavy dragon's tail pulled her under the waves, and she kept sinking. From twenty feet below the surface, Tonya looked up at Anderson calmly treading water. Did he know she was in trouble?

And if he wasn't worried, should she be?

Kicking hard and pulling with her arms, she dragged her heavy tail to the surface. Her back arched with pain, but she controlled this scaly body, nobody else. She slowed, rolled onto her back, and blew out a plume of wet air. The visualization, the potion, and the joy of swimming had culminated in a complete transformation.

It was awkward to move four enormous legs through the water, dragging her tail and wings, but Tonya was a water baby. Years of swimming had trained her mind to search for efficiencies.

When she tucked her wings against her body, it reduced drag and she went faster. Her front claws out front helped to stabilize and steer. Instead of kicking, she held her legs and body straight, like a torpedo, and propelled herself with powerful tail swishes. This sleek, scaly body cut through the ocean currents. With a whoop she dove to the bottom, planted her feet and pushed off, lashing her powerful tail until she breached the water and sailed into the air like a dolphin. *Incredible!*

With flicks of her powerful tail, she swam figure eights on the surface. *How's that, Hatch?*

It was just like him to go silent in her moment of triumph. His sole aim was to make Tonya doubt herself and isolate her from her friends. She understood that now. Driving away Drake, shaming her, making her steal. The scheming narcissist wanted to break her and claim total control.

She lifted her snout, inhaled, then dove, letting her tail propel her better than a motor. On a whim, she flapped her wings, and then she was flying underwater! Down, down, down, and then she used her tail to execute a tight turn and raced upward. When she surfaced, a giant red dragon came up for air beside her, dipped its jaws back under the waves, and spit a deluge of water in her face.

She spluttered and roared, but before she could retaliate, he swam for the bottom and the race was on!

And so they played, diving, chasing, and racing like otters until Tonya heaved up on the shore, exhausted. She'd had enough.

Time to switch back into her human form, but when she concentrated on becoming Tonya, nothing happened.

Nice try, puny human, but it's done. I'm a dragon forever and control will be mine.

His laughter echoed in her ears as she blacked out.

28

PLASTIC STARS GLEAMED IN the painted blue sky above Tonya's head like a bedroom from childhood. *Somebody else's childhood.* Her hands explored the stiff sheet at her sides covering the hard metal ... gurney?

In the hospital, in jail. She was still in the National police station somewhere. Tonya sat up, letting her feet dangle over the side of the gurney while she got her bearings.

The room looked like a pediatrician's waiting room with toys scattered on the floor, but a colorful volcano mural decorated with pink clouds looked familiar. So did the sandy beach painted on the wall behind her. The door in the mural swung open.

"Good. You're awake." Under the fluorescent lights, Sheriff Anderson looked smaller and less heroic than in her dreams.

Was that all they were? The vivid landscape with plasticine-bright volcano and golden shore were hallucinations brought on by Paloma's IV injections and inspired by the images on these walls. But the experience had felt real. She'd never learned how to do something in a dream before, and the events tied together chronologically. In dreams, things just happened without cause and effect.

"What did you do to me?"

Anderson didn't answer immediately. "Your time's up tomorrow, and you're the lead suspect with motive, means, and opportunity. If you can't give me an alibi, I'll have to arrest you."

"What gives you the right to play with my head? You're worse than Hatch!"

"You're welcome for trying to save you." He scratched the stubble on his chin. "How much do you remember?"

"You were there, so you tell me."

"Tonya!" Helen came in behind the sheriff. "I've been so worried about you."

Helen? Was the whole town in on this? "You were worried so the logical thing to do was to let him drug me and run me through some kind of magical dragon initiation ceremony, so he could question me once I broke down?"

"Not quite." To his credit, the sheriff couldn't meet her eye. "But I hoped that if you integrated your personality with Hatch, you'd be able to remember enough to provide an alibi. National uses magically enhanced hypnotism to help witnesses remember what they saw."

"That's his excuse." Tonya glared at Helen. "What's yours?"

"If you can't regain control, Hatch will take over your mind unless ..."

"She can't kill him." Anderson leveled his gaze at Helen, then back at Tonya. "Neither can you."

"Even if Hatch erases her personality," Helen's voice broke, "and I lose my little girl?"

"From National's point of view, this dimension is overrun with humans. If Tonya kills Hatch, an intelligent member of an ancient and rare magical race, she will be guilty of genocide as well as murder."

29

Sheriff Anderson led Tonya out of the colorful waiting room and through the halls of the police station to the booking area, where she reclaimed her possessions and dressed for the outside world. Paloma Alvarez hadn't pressed charges, probably to avoid being charged with kidnapping.

In a daze, Tonya emerged from the red tent into the dark and Loon Lake's icy wind. Her stomach growled because she hadn't eaten lunch, and it was past time for dinner.

On the walk back to campus, the cold gnawed at her toes right through her winter boots. Magically enhanced hypnosis hadn't proved her innocence, but it had failed to prove her guilt, so they'd released her on the condition that Helen would watch over her. At the first twinge of transformation, Tonya was supposed to text Helen, who would rush to Tonya's side and use her ability to charm beasts to subdue Hatch.

Good luck with that.

If she was honest, Tonya didn't think Helen could control Hatch either, but her release gave her a chance to ferret out the truth. The sheriff's hypnosis trick didn't stir up new memories. All Tonya had were questions. If Hatch hadn't made her kill Donna Ashton, why had she awoken at the scene of the crime? And who killed Donna?

At a loss, her nerves raw with everything Anderson had put her through, Tonya's fingers itched to dial Drake. It would be such a comfort to hear his voice and pretend everything was normal.

But anything she said would be too weird. No one would understand the hallucinogenic ordeal they'd put her through. It was an unforgivable invasion of privacy. Anderson was evil to manipulate her like that, and she could never forgive Helen for letting him violate her mind. Swinging her arms and marching helped dissipate her anger, but they had betrayed her.

Back at the Mackenzie residence, she grabbed a wedge of pizza from the cafeteria and gazed out the window, letting her mind drift away from unhappy thoughts. As she stared at the moonlight reflecting on the lake, she wondered if any part of the dream had been real. Could she truly transform into a dragon and swim in the frigid water, or would she drown? Could she conquer her fear of heights and fly?

After the meal, the thought of her cramped room repelled her. Instead, she took the elevator to the top floor and the emergency staircase to the roof. Frosty air filled her lungs as she surveyed the snow sparkling around the lit path running along the lake shore. When Hatch was restless, he liked to stand here, but now that she could remember shifting in her dreams, the sky tugged at her too. She yearned to fly away from the mess she was in, letting her worries shrink on the ground.

Like it was nothing, the change began. Her bones cracked as they migrated to new positions. *Too fast!* Her scream deepened to a roar as her flesh expanded, her limbs morphed, and she sprouted wings, pearly scales, and a row of dorsal fins.

Panting and lightheaded in her giant body, Tonya launched herself into the chilly sky and dropped. Pointing her nose down, she flapped hard into a dive then turned and soared up, breaching the clouds on her way southwest. Without thinking, Tonya aimed for the haze of light pollution on the horizon. Dad had moved to Toronto to escape the chaos and Old Family conflicts that had ruined his marriage. She should go see him before Christmas. Really, she should.

But first there was someone she needed to see even more. Flying, even with a strong tailwind, would take hours, but time wasn't the problem. How was she going to recognize the house from the air? Loon Lake shrank behind her as Tonya sailed over farms, dirt roads, and scrubby forests that were nearly invisible in the dark.

30

NEARLY TWO AND A half hours later, Tonya soared over the sparsely lit cluster of farms, orchards, and country businesses that ringed Greater Toronto. The streetlights on Steeles Avenue flickered past in a blink. She had to be close. Drake lived in the east end of Scarborough, the easternmost part of the city.

Dragons have excellent night vision, and remembered the landmarks. A deep ravine with a creek separated Scarborough from Pickering, close to his house. It was near Lake Ontario, perched on a hill overlooking Rouge Beach. The house had been built before the commuter train station or the nearby national park, where Drake had once taken her for a bike ride. Holding hands, they'd eaten a picnic on the sandy beach, watching sailboats drift across Lake Ontario while locals cast fishing lines into the lily-covered inlet.

There it was! Glowing under the moonlight, the ice-covered inlet looked like a vast pond where white swans gathered, some sitting, others standing on partially submerged sheets of ice.

With her built-in dragon furnace, the icy wind didn't bother Tonya. After circling the pond, she got her bearings from the streetlights along Lawrence Avenue and headed west until she spotted familiar Christmas lights on a house perched above the street. Dormant vines and pine trees blocked her view of the yard, so she landed in front of the house, shying away from the streetlights. Her claws dug into the icy road, the thin skin between them tingling as rock salt lodged between her talons.

Had anyone seen her?

Running between multimillion-dollar homes, the steep road looked deserted. It was evening, past rush hour. With a glance over her shoulder, she slipped beside the house and into the backyard. Vines tangled over the tall wire fence, and an enormous pine tree shielded her from view. This was the perfect vantage point to make sure Drake was okay.

That was the reason she was here, right? To check on him, to make sure he was safe? She absolutely had not come to spy on him or reassure herself that he was just as miserable without her as she was without him.

She crept closer to the house. Almost there. Almost close enough to peer into the windows—if only she could slow her breathing and stop thinking predatory thoughts about the fuzzy black rodents curled up in their leafy nest at the top of the tree.

Squirrels!

Tonya's tail lashed back and forth. A raccoon in a neighbor's tree chittered a warning that sent the rest of the nighttime animals fleeing.

She'd teach that little snitch a lesson and roast him alive! Tonya paced forward, following the smell of that raccoon and its garbage bag breath.

A porcupine cowered under the deck on the side of the house—as if she couldn't scoop him up with one swipe of her claws. Tonya crept forward, enjoying the soundless padding of her feet on snow. Her chest puffed out knowing that, despite her enormous size, she could walk as silently as a cat.

This was Drake's dining room window. He sat with his family, enjoying a holiday meal. Candlelight danced on their smiling faces. Everything was peaceful and joyous—except Drake wasn't alone. A slender beauty with blonde ringlets held his hand and whispered in his ear.

Drake already had a new girl? And she was meeting his family?

A mournful roar tore from her throat. He must have met the blonde in the summer or fall, when Tonya had been avoiding him. He was a jerk and a cheat—but she was the one who had pushed him away and kept him there.

Tonya's tears pocked the snow as they rolled down her scaly snout.

But then, her tears stopped. Her snout was shrinking.

No. This couldn't be happening.

Desperately, she tried to think dragony thoughts, but all she could picture was Drake cuddling up to his pretty new girlfriend. Breaking up had been Tonya's idea, and she should be happy he wasn't alone, but all she could think of was how much she had lost.

Tonya stood on the snow, a mess of shivering human nakedness, just as Drake glanced out the window. He leaned forward, his eyes popped—and Tonya fled.

Every time she tried to transform, thoughts of Drake brought her back to humanity until she wanted to give up and walk home on bare feet. If she didn't leave soon, Drake's neighbors would call the police to report a naked madwoman wandering through the backyards of their upscale community.

Drake's coming. I heard somebody throw a bolt on the back door, Hatch's tone was polite. *Allow me?*

No thanks. Her inner parasite was up to something. Let him drive again, and she'd black out and wake up in a ditch.

He sounded hurt. *That's not fair.*

What's not fair is you eavesdropping on my thoughts when I can't hear yours.

Fine. I hope your ex calls the cops on you for stalking him naked.

When Hatch put it that way, she couldn't refuse.

The transformation was painful, made worse by her need to stay quiet, but shifting with Hatch's cooperation was quick. Heat radiated from her belly to the tips of her silvery wings. Three running steps and a push-off sent her into the air, flapping hard until the grid of streets and leafy suburbs below shrank to toy size.

If anybody noticed an object without lights above Toronto, they would assume it was a high-flying Canada goose. To stay hidden, Hatch weaved through low-flying clouds looking up now and then to avoid collisions.

In the past, whenever Hatch forced her on night flights, Tonya closed her eyes and concentrated on not getting dizzy while he tormented her with barrel rolls, steep dives, and stalling maneuvers.

On this flight, in partnership with Hatch, she enjoyed gliding through the air, wings flapping in harmonious rhythm. Dragon vision gave her confidence and flying felt natural. A chance to let her mind rest and enjoy the wind on her face and the heat in her belly.

You try, Hatch urged.

As easily as thought, she banked right or left. She could speed up or glide at will, measuring her progress against the farmlands and forests hurtling below her.

In a moment of exhilaration, she dove. The shredded wheat rolls of hay on a farmer's field came into sharp focus before she shot back up to the clouds, roaring with joy.

What have I been trying to tell you? Hatch asked. *Flying is fun.*

They took a turn above Loon Lake Village where revelers packed the streets. Somebody set off a magical firework that exploded next to her sensitive snout, knocking her off course. She regained equilibrium, roaring and breathing fire, her mind filled with murderous intentions.

As she banked and came back to locate the culprit, a different tourist shot Roman candles at her. They went off in her face.

Pop! Pop! Pop!

Shock waves jostled the air, and her temper flared. She dove, flames emerging from her mouth, only to abort at the last minute—filled with shame.

Since when did she run on anger? Was she turning into Hatch?

Below her, stupid revelers shot charmed potato guns at each other, the starchy projectiles turning and weaving through the air like self-guided spud missiles. It was like a riot of practical jokers, and she coasted lower to take in the spectacle.

With dragon vision, she spotted Stephen Ashton cast a disease spell on a group of tourists who staggered away barfing. Disease curses were his specialty, but it surprised Tonya to see Stephen ditch the pursuit of pleasure and designer loot to help with crowd control. Marvin must have showered his brother with praise for his massive strength and terrifying ability to inflict illness to get him to pitch in.

Without Mayor Donna's powers at command, Ashton Security would have trouble clearing hundreds of drunken pranksters from Loon Lake Village, because they had no way to neutralize their powers. Worse yet, there was time for the tourists to figure that out with five more days until Christmas. National had to let the cruise ship go and return the tourists to their families, or they'd riot.

She sailed over the invisible wall and headed for campus.

31

It was late by the time she set her claws down on the Mackenzie dorm roof. With her new dragon strength, she forced the door open and took the stairs to her floor. Back in her room, she noticed Zain had texted an invitation to a private screening of the Digital Ninja's new horror film. It was a rough cut with basic sound for the following night.

Drake was lost to her forever, but she never wanted to lose Zain and the Ninjas. She inhaled through her nose and exhaled slowly before texting Zain back.

—*Is Priya coming to the screening?*

—*Yes & Drake*

Awkward.

Another guy would be mad at the way she'd dumped him. And if that guy wanted the means to avenge himself, she'd laid it bare before him. Literally.

But Drake had always treated her well. He wouldn't distribute pics of her naked shame, but it would hurt too much to see disappointment in his eyes. He must think she was desperate and coming unglued to stalk him in the raw.

—*I can't come. Can't explain why.*

—*Grace was brilliant. You have to see her starring role.*

She couldn't. She just couldn't. Tonya had a murderer to catch and a reputation to rebuild. Watching a movie wouldn't help her do either, although it would be nice to have the Ninja's help. She never would have caught Jack Waldock's killer without them, and here she was trying to do everything alone. It was a mistake—but the embarrassment!

For hours Tonya lay on her thin mattress, staring at the ceiling. She couldn't face seeing Drake or his new girl with the pretty blonde hair. It would be too humiliating.

But living on the same campus, she wouldn't be able to dodge Drake forever. Could she? No. She could pull off the bandage fast or slow, there was no avoiding the pain.

When she texted Zain to confirm she'd be there, he sent a pic of the movie poster featuring Grace in a heroic pose and Zain in a cheesy skintight elf costume.

How could she possibly miss that?

32

THIS LATE MOST STUDENTS would be sleeping, but Tonya knew Priya better than that. By lamplight, she rode her bike along the waterfront path to the art studio where a warm glow spilled out of the two-story windows. She leaned her bike against the dark side of the building.

It wouldn't be an easy conversation. Her bestie might be angry after Tonya ran off during the Christmas movie without explaining, but what other practitioner could she trust? Helen maybe, but if her birth mom had been spying for National, what other secrets was she keeping? With the way Helen charmed animals, and let Sheriff Anderson invade her mind, Tonya didn't know how much to trust her.

Nobody answered the first time she knocked, so Tonya knocked louder.

Wearing a welding helmet with the visor tipped open, Priya flung open the door. "Wait, I still have twenty minutes."

"Sorry." Behind Priya, Tonya glimpsed her friend's latest sculpture, eight feet of metal supports and trusses. A ladder stood next to it, beside the huge gas canister Priya used for welding.

"This is a surprise." Priya lifted off the helmet and shook out her pigtails. "Are we on speaking terms?"

"Yeah. I'm sorry about running out on Movie Night."

"And then not calling," Priya said.

"That too."

"Come in."

"It can wait." Tonya sat on a bench at the back of the studio. "I don't want to waste your studio time." Priya earned her time by working for Loon Lake's creepy ghost librarian.

"Sit. Talk." Priya sat beside Tonya. "What's going on?"

It came out in a rush. "The sheriff from National thinks I killed Donna."

Priya opened her arms, and Tonya crumbled into them. "Nobody could think that."

The dragon in Tonya appreciated the smoky odor of Priya's singed coverall. "He has evidence. You know the blackouts I've been having?"

Priya nodded.

"I woke up on the beach near the mayor's body."

"Do you think Roberto manipulated you?" A stormy expression crossed Priya's brow.

"No."

"Tell Drake to come back to Loon Lake. He wants to help."

"Until I can prove I'm innocent, he has to stay away from me. It's the only way to protect him."

"But I'm dispensable?" Priya grinned, giving Tonya a playful shove.

"You have powers and connections with the Old Families. You can defend yourself." It wasn't flattery.

"Protecting Drake might make you lose him."

"If I'm a murderer, I deserve to."

"Stop that right now." Priya shrugged out of the coverall and took her phone from her pocket. "I'm going to text him to come in the morning."

"No!" Tonya grabbed for the phone.

Priya fled up the ladder. "You need him. Give me one good reason I shouldn't bring him back."

It came out in a jumble. Hatch tormenting her and getting stronger every day. The way he forced her to steal the ring. The blackouts and night flights she only found out about because her stomach was full of vermin. The breakup. After keeping secrets for so long, it was a relief to spill everything to her best friend.

"They took me in for questioning, because they think I killed Donna. Sheriff Anderson knows about Hatch inside me and him taking over. He suspects me, and if I can't give him an alibi tomorrow, National will arrest me and put me away for a very long time."

"I don't believe you killed anyone."

"A dragon killed the mayor. I found the body and saw the claw marks—which also means I have no alibi. Either I find out who else did it, or Anderson will arrest me for killing her."

"Tell me how I can help."

"What if Hatch made me black out and do it?"

"You aren't capable of murder, no matter what else is inside you."

"But Hatch ..."

"... could make you steal a ring, eat a few mice..." Priya made a face. "That I believe—but you're still Tonya. You're the girl who put up with Marta and the Mod bullies instead of fighting back with your powers."

Maybe she was right. Tonya blinked back tears. Priya had to be right.

"And if I ever meet this Hatch ..." Priya drew a finger across her neck making a ridiculous choking sound.

Tonya grinned. Despite everything at risk, talking to Priya made her feel at home. "I have until tomorrow to prove I didn't do it, but all the evidence points at me. What if I blacked out and Hatch was able to make me do it because I hated Donna and subconsciously wanted revenge?"

"Stop beating yourself up." Priya rested her hands on Tonya's shoulders. "It's like you've become your own bully."

"No, that's Hatch's job. He's always pestering me, except—and this is weird—since Anderson questioned me, he hasn't said a word."

"That's good, right? He's stopped bossing you around."

"Maybe, but the sheriff has telepathy. Anderson and Helen can hear Hatch when he talks to me. I think Hatch is lying low because he murdered Donna and doesn't want to say anything incriminating."

"How well do you really know Helen? I know she's your mother, but she left you for her sister to raise, and she practiced necromancy. Not the actions of an innocent woman."

"Helen didn't do it."

"She can charm animals. What if somebody paid her to make a dragon attack Mayor Ashton because she built the wall? Or Helen could have done it for revenge. She and Mayor Ashton hated each other."

"Helen's a good person who got scapegoated." She didn't want to hear any more. Priya wasn't going to help, so Tonya went for the door.

"Don't be offended." Priya followed Tonya. "I'm brainstorming. Who else could have done it?"

Tonya wished she knew. "Helen can influence animals, but right before the murder, I admitted to Helen that Hatch was controlling me. She would never commit a crime in a way that made me look guilty."

"Who does that leave?"

"It feels like the whole town. There are so many protestors who hated the mayor's new policies, but it's tricky to speak to Mundanes. If they've been in and out of Loon Lake Village, they may have trouble recollecting things. A lot of them had their memories wiped after the Jack Waldock fiasco."

"You think a Mundane killed Donna?"

"A Mundane wouldn't know enough to fake a dragon attack. This was the work of the Old Families or a practitioner from out of town. It would be nice to find a Mundane or practitioner who saw something. Sheriff Anderson has canvassed Loon Lake Village and the City of Loon Lake but found no witnesses or evidence to help narrow things down. That's why I'm here."

It was a big ask, but Priya could visit the one place where Tonya would never be welcome.

"Could you ask around for me in the cemetery?"

33

Sheriff Anderson would be coming after Tonya, but she still couldn't name the mayor's killer. Too many Loon Lakers had motive leaving her baffled, but as she lay in bed, staring out the window into the darkness, she smiled. She, Tonya Jones, once the butt of high school bullies, could turn herself into a terrifying, fire-breathing dragon!

Time to get up and find that killer—before the sheriff found her. She grabbed her shower stuff and padded down the hall in stolen pink flip-flops. At this time of day, there would be plenty of hot water, and she did her best thinking while washing her hair.

The dorm had a row of individual cubicles with lockable doors and hooks inside to hang your stuff out of the spray. Tonya pushed the button and waited for the water to heat up. As she got wet, she pondered which dragon had murdered Donna Ashton. During her trip to Toronto, and on all those flights around Loon Lake, she'd never seen or heard of an unknown dragon. They were extremely rare, like shifters. What did the sheriff say? It had been ten years since he'd met another dragon woman.

Tonya massaged her favorite strawberry shampoo into her scalp. Its sweetness smelled too strong to her dragon senses. She'd have to buy something unscented, something she couldn't smell for miles.

Miles.

If there was another dragon in Loon Lake, she would have seen it or sniffed it from miles away. Negative evidence was proof. Tonya had smelled traces of dragon on the corpse, so if it wasn't Hatch, Flores did it. The murderer could control dragons.

The water shut itself off, and she toweled dry, happy to eliminate most of the residents of Loon Lake. It didn't exonerate her but made her a prime suspect—until she figured out who did it and proved it to the sheriff. How hard could it be with a small pool of suspects?

With her hair wrapped in a towel, Tonya whistled to herself as she came out of the shower—until she saw the sheriff and two cops with a battering ram waiting outside her room.

"Sheriff, you don't need to arrest me. I've had a breakthrough!"

They came after her, but Anderson waved them to slow down. "Don't bluff."

"You've watched me transform, so you can trust my dragon senses." Tonya set down her shower stuff and slipped out of her sandals. "I didn't smell Hatch on the mayor's body. It was another dragon. Go sniff for yourself. I'm innocent."

"She's buried." He nodded to the officers who surged forward. "Time's up. Keep your hands where we can see them and don't resist."

The cops advanced on her calmly, inevitable as death and final exams. Searching for options, Tonya noticed a door left ajar.

She ducked through the gap, locking up behind her. To the sound of shouts and hammering fists, Tonya threw open the window. *Hatch, are you with me?*

In moments, the police would batter down the door. She perched on the ledge, made sure her phone was in her bathrobe pocket, and used the tie to fasten it around her neck. As she braced herself against the window frame, pain staggered her, causing her to slip toward the edge. Her body changed too fast, ballooning outward like one big nerve on fire in a huge scaly embrace of pain that wouldn't let go until she leaped from the window spreading her wings.

34

TONYA FLEW ABOVE THE clouds wondering how to hide from Sheriff Anderson who could transform into a much more powerful dragon. If she circled too long, pondering the question, he'd catch her. She needed to hide somewhere National couldn't go. Private property owned by the kind of paranoid nuts or incurable rebels who'd rather trust their safety to a dog and a shotgun so they could break the rules in their own domain. The kind of people who felt themselves above the law and lived behind a concrete wall topped with broken glass ...

Won't they be surprised? She flattened her wings against her body, hoping nobody saw her dive, a pearlescent streak of white in the gray winter sky.

Tonya landed in a patch of snow and leaves against the back wall of the Ashton's mansion. She willed herself to transform back into a human.

No. Hatch whined like a spoiled five-year-old. *I wasn't finished flying.*

Tonya didn't want to transform either. It was going to hurt, but to hide from Anderson, she had to get inside the house.

Please, Hatch. I have to fit through the door, or we won't be safe.

The Ashtons had flouted the law against magic use for years before Mayor Donna Ashton repealed the rules. They would be equipped with modern counter surveillance measures and powerful wards to keep out prying eyes.

Fine. But first promise me—

Shhh! She heard the Ashton Brothers through the walls. *Don't change us back yet.*

She could hear best in dragon form, and those boys sounded pretty angry. What were they arguing about? Tonya got close to a window and peeped in. They were right there! Marvin, who never showed emotion in public, was red in the face from shouting at Stephen.

"Rainbow slime! Your excuse is rainbow slime!"

Stephen, who cultivated an arrogant, superior attitude in public, hung his head. His big shoulders rounded forward like a scolded puppy.

If only she could hear more, but the glass was two panes thick, and Marvin had stopped yelling. His voice dropped to the kind of intense tones that expressed anger under extreme restraint. Whatever the reason he was telling his brother off, Marvin was deadly serious.

Tonya tried to read their lips but couldn't. Maybe Marta knew what was going on. Tonya gripped the side of the building and heaved herself up, her claws and tail proving excellent tools for climbing.

Gripping onto window ledges, balconies, and downspouts, Tonya made her way around the second floor, looking into the bedrooms to find Marta. She had made it around two sides of the building when an icy blue ball of power crashed into the wall beside her head. Strangely, the bricks remained unharmed, but her claws went numb. They released their grip on the façade sending her falling.

35

Priya should have been sleeping in to celebrate the school holidays, but Tonya was desperate. So here she was, early Saturday morning, trudging through crisp frozen leaves past hundred-year-old monuments dusted in snow. Her objective was a large mausoleum in the Old Family section of Loon Lake Cemetery, near the burned-out stump of the Three-Century Ash.

What a pain. If her friend had refrained from arson in the cemetery, Tonya could question the ghosts herself, and Priya could be having brunch in Toronto, eating homemade treats with her cousins.

Adding to the insult, Tonya had provided a long list of Pure and Trad surnames. "Don't disturb these ghosts." As if Priya needed reminding about ghost-witch diplomacy! She'd been working for Loon Lake's ghost librarian long enough to respect the dead. It was a Loon Lake tradition.

On the emerald lawn, no grave in the Old Family section lacked a bouquet of fresh or silk flowers. She recognized the Greek-inspired mausoleum on a rise overlooking the lake. Most communities reserved lakefront property for the living, but here the dead had clout. You could see it in the expensive marble, Corinthian columns, and decorative carvings adorning the sepulcher. The iron gate opened without a creak, and she descended into the crypt.

Office furniture and technology from various eras cluttered the dim underground headquarters of the Fading Times. The newspaper started in the 1940s, and there was little evidence they'd thrown away anything since then. Phantom inkwells and ghostly antique cameras didn't take up real space and could be kept in overlapping stacks against the side walls. At rows of diverse desks, hacks wearing fedoras and plucky Girl Fridays with hourglass figures tapped away at manual typewriters. The earnest newspapermen of the 1950s wore brush cuts, their hats adorned with press cards. Closer to the glassed-in editor's office, women with padded shoulders and big hair wrote with word processors and answered pagers.

The editor's door stood ajar, so she stepped into the office expecting Matheson, the grizzled editor.

"Hey toots!"

"Johnny?" That was a surprise. It was the ghost newspaper boy she hadn't laid eyes on since the summer. "I'm happy to see you."

"Likewise." He waggled his eyebrows suggestively. "Shut the door if you want to get even happier."

"Incorrigible. You haven't changed."

"Haven't I?" He stood, turning this way and that so she could appreciate his snappy suspenders and pinstriped pants tailored to his ten-year-old frame. "When they made me editor, I finally got out of short pants. Get a load of this." He put on a fedora instead of the newsboy cap Priya remembered.

"Congratulations." She held her hand out to shake.

"Nice try, toots." He whisked an icy ghost hand through hers. "What brings you here?"

"Have you been following the Donna Ashton case?"

"That you gotta ask cuts me to the quick. Don't you read my paper?"

"Sorry."

"Relax, toots. I understand. These days, even ghosts prefer to watch their news on the Old Family app. If there's no moving pictures, they're not interested. It's getting so the new dead aren't lining up to become reporters either. They want their own shows on YouTube—it's a low-down shame." He shook his head and sat behind his desk. "Whaddaya need, baby doll?"

"We were wondering if you or any of the ghosts heard rumors about Donna's death. The Mundane police assumed it was a bear, and National is rushing to close the case and move on."

"I haven't heard much." He tipped back the brim of his ghostly fedora and leaned back in his chair. "Who does National suspect?"

She had been expecting this question. A newshound hunts information. He doesn't give it away for free. "Tonya and Helen, but Marta suspects her father, who came back to claim the house."

"Interesting." He laced his hands behind his neck and tilted his head up. "The dad angle would be juicy, but he had no reason to kill his wife. I saw a copy of the deed, and Donna never owned the house. Sheriff Anderson cleared Helen, but she could fake an alibi by charming any Mundane to think they were together that night. Tonya's up to something with her sneaky mom-slash-aunt. They're powerful witches with revenge motives and a history of scheming together. Helen could make a bear attack. We saw her make an angry dragon bow to her on the beach at Donna's inauguration picnic."

"They're innocent. Don't you suspect anybody else?" The interview with Johnny wasn't helping. All she'd done was draw attention to Tonya and Helen. "Please, didn't some member of the ghost community see anything? They found Donna's body on the beach between the public swimming area and the Mod boathouse. Do you have informants haunting the beach?"

"Maybe, but Tonya should be here herself to trade information, tit for tat. But she's too scared to enter the cemetery, and she thinks it's fair to waste my time and yours. Shouldn't you be carving your next prize-winning sculpture?"

"I can investigate better than Tonya because I can see all the ghosts, not just the ones who want me to see them."

"Is that right?" Johnny faded.

"Wait! Don't go."

He popped into view, glowing brighter than before. "It wouldn't hurt to have some humility. You also see ghosts only when they want you to see them."

"But Tonya—"

"Has made a lot of enemies."

Priya couldn't deny it. "You've been very helpful." She stood. Or, if not helpful, at least honest.

He walked her to the door. "Talk to the Wilsons. Their family plot overlooks the beach. In life, Mother Wilson used to spy on the neighbors from behind her front curtains. In death, she's an even bigger busybody with nothing else to do."

"I appreciate the tip."

He threw an arm around her waist and pinched her butt—which felt like getting poked by an ice cube.

"Johnny!" She delivered a slap that went right through his head.

"Sorry, toots. Couldn't help myself." He hung his head like a little boy.

By the time Johnny gave her directions to the Wilson plot, she had almost forgiven the antique rascal. Charming, excitable, and career focused like her, it made Priya happy to see the 1940s paperboy make good. His flirting was irritating, but the old-school sexist probably thought he was flattering her.

"Walk me over? You could introduce me to the Wilsons."

"Love to toots, but there's no time. Since ghosts discovered smartphones, I lose a reporter every month. I feel like the chief cook and bottle washer now." He handed her a glowing piece of paper. "If Mrs. Wilson can't help, proceed with caution."

It was a list entitled "Do not Disturb" which lined up precisely with Tonya's.

"Don't worry. I won't go near any Pure graves."

The Wilsons had a reddish granite stone on a rise that gave them a view over the cemetery and the part of the beach near the scene of the crime. To grease the wheels, Priya had brought a bag of ghost library books as an offering. The Librarian, not knowing who Priya would speak to, had provided a variety of genres in glowing paperback format.

"Mrs. Wilson?"

A glowing figure rose out of the ground and floated in the shade of a towering pine tree. "Yes?"

It surprised Priya to see her youthful face, gingham sundress, and wedge sandals.

"Who are you?"

"I'm sorry to disturb you. My name's Priya, and I'm here to ask—"

"Oh, the Ghost Librarian talks about you. Welcome to my little domain." The young woman stretched out her arm to encompass the view. "Call me Angela."

"Thanks." Priya noticed the ghost held a baby on her hip. "And who's this little sweetie?" She moved to pull back the blanket and see its face, but Angela shifted it out of her reach.

"I love my little Cutie. But where's Daddy?" she asked the swaddled babe.

Forgetting Priya, she strode to the edge of the cemetery lawn and used two hands to peek through ghostly blinds that only appeared when her hands touched them. She sighed. "Working, always working." Turning back she asked Priya, "What were we saying?"

"There was a murder on the beach. Johnny thought you or someone in your family might have seen something."

"Yes, it was strange. I saw Donna on the beach carrying that big gem on a stick thing she likes to wave around."

The Staff of Storms. "Was anyone with her?"

"She was waiting for somebody." The ghost put the baby over her shoulder and looked Priya in the eye. "It was important. She was pacing, and she was so nervous that, well, you know those long blood-red fingernails of hers?" She paused for effect, enjoying a chance to dish some hot gossip. "Well, she was biting them. Donna Ashton biting her nails! She must spend a hundred a month for mani-pedis."

Angela didn't need to be bribed with library books; she loved to tell all. "Who did she meet?"

"A ghost, very faded. They argued for a while, but when it left and she didn't, I figured she was waiting for somebody else."

Priya nodded encouragingly. "And?"

"I don't know. After that, Donna walked farther along the beach and the Mod boathouse blocked my view. Next, I heard they found her in the morning. What a dreadful business."

Priya would have said a ghastly business. Was that insulting? "Could you tell whether Donna went into Ted Kwok's campground when she disappeared?"

The phantom shrugged. "I can't leave the cemetery and traipse around the countryside. Once the old ghost left, I kind of lost interest because I had this little one to look after." She nuzzled the top of the baby's head and kissed it.

Priya swallowed. Had her baby died? "I didn't know ghosts could have babies."

"It's not mine." She let the infant grab her finger. "You're here on loan, aren't you, cutie patootie?"

Alive or not, the spectral infant gurgled and cooed like the real thing. "May I?" Priya held out her hands.

Mrs. Wilson gave her the bundle, which chilled the flannel blanket. When she held it up to her face to say hello, a long hairy limb reached out and pulled her braid.

"Hey!" Now it had both braids in its glowing hands. "Call off your monkey!"

"Oh, dear." Mrs. Wilson tried to take back her bundle, but the athletic creature kicked away the blanket and shot up the pine tree. "Come back, Slayer!"

"Is that his name?"

"I think so. You'd have to check with the ringmaster buried in the new section. Sometimes I monkey sit." She waved up the tree. "When the ringmaster passed on, Slayer escaped the circus to visit his ghost in the cemetery."

"They still have circuses?"

"You tell me." She shrugged. "I've been monkey sitting for eighty years."

36

Tonya plummeted headfirst.

Hatch! Help!

Relax, puny human.

Taking control, he spread their wings wide, slowed their fall, and executed a midair spin that landed them on their feet. Curiosity tempted her to cling to the wall, eavesdropping for further clues, but there were strong wards in place.

Before the Ashton's defences hurled another freeze ball, she took a running start and flew above the clouds until she reached the cemetery where she hid in a huge mausoleum near the entrance. Nobody would look for her there, and in dragon form, vengeful spirits wouldn't recognize her.

Priya was supposed to question the ghosts this morning, but her friend wasn't a morning person. Tonya could be chilling her scales in the damp, cold mausoleum for a long time.

At least it smells like mice.

Thanks, Hatch. National wants to arrest me, Sheriff Anderson thinks I'm a murderer, and the ghosts would attack if they knew it was me—but at least the mausoleum smells like mice!

You're welcome.

Tonya couldn't tell if he was being sarcastic, but she sure was. A strong shiver sent a ripple through her tail, scraping it against the wall. Unless she figured out who killed the mayor soon, National would leave her to rot in a cell much like this fusty mausoleum.

While she watched for Priya, Tonya yearned to get her phone out of the bathrobe that hung around her neck. She needed to apologize to Grace that she would have to miss the Ninja's movie premiere. Despite her flights and near misses, the phone remained in the pocket of the bathrobe, but it was useless in her dragon claws.

The sun shone high in the chilly sky by the time Tonya spied Priya approaching the Western Gate. Tonya wanted to call out, but dragons could only bellow, hiss, or breathe fire. She could transform, but, considering how much the local ghosts hated her, it was better to get outside the gates first.

As Priya left the cemetery, Tonya bounded out of the mausoleum and caught up with her on the grass outside the gate. So as not to frighten her Priya, Tonya threw herself onto her back and thrashed back and forth, scratching her scales against the turf like a dog.

This was supposed to demonstrate that she was playful, not a bloodthirsty, flame-throwing Priya-eating beast. It also scratched part of her back beside the dorsal spines that was always itchy and difficult to reach.

Priya stopped in her tracks and slowly backed away.

"Don't go back in the cemetery!"

Tonya's voice came out a meaningless roar, but brave Priya stood her ground. She eyed Tonya where she lay, claws up and tail switching playfully.

"That's you, isn't it?"

It was the first time Tonya had spoken to Priya in dragon form. Tonya nodded her head. *Too bad she didn't have telepathy.*

Priya looked around. "Oh, I get it. You're hiding from the ghosts."

Tonya sat up on her haunches and nodded again.

Priya asked, "Aren't you going to become human?"

Tonya shook her head slowly. It was hard to get used to her long neck.

Priya thought for a beat. "All right then, here's what I found out. Are you listening?"

Tonya nodded. *Good old unflappable Priya.* Tonya would give her a great big hug—if it wouldn't crush her to death.

"The ghosts told me Donna Ashton came to the beach and met with an angry ghost the afternoon she was killed. My witness couldn't see anything else because the mayor walked along the beach to the far side of the boathouse."

"Oh, and this is kind of weird, but might be related ... when Zain and Grace were on the island, they found an animal skeleton. But they won't tell me—or anyone—the details. I begged them to tell me, but they said 'spoilers.' If you want to know what they found, you have to come to their film debut tonight. You were coming anyway, right?"

Tonya tried to shrug, but the movement went into her wings.

"No, wait. You *are* coming now, aren't you?"

Tonya nodded. It would be risky with Anderson looking for her, but if she arrived after the lights went out and left early, she should be able to talk to Zain unseen.

37

Tonya met Priya on her floor in the common area to learn what the ghosts knew. Once Tonya had heard all Priya's stories, the friends parted ways to get ready for the Ninja's premiere.

For Zain and Grace's big moment, Tonya chose a sparkly blue top and her best jeans. The outfit looked okay with the white hair death magic gave her, but it was time to update her style. Helen sported necro hair like a personal flag of rebellion, but Tonya was too young for white hair. Restoring the natural red color was impossible, but she could dye it a fun shade for New Year's Eve—assuming she caught the murderer and there was something to celebrate.

The Hub Pub, usually quiet during the holidays, was full of newlyweds and gray-haired couples fresh off the cruise ship. Out-of-town practitioners occupied every booth and barstool, and they lined the stairs to the basement room where the Digital Ninjas held their meetings.

Students and curious tourists packed the clubhouse. Near the front, Tonya spotted Priya, Grace, and Drake with the blonde from Toronto in the front row. *Ugh.* Tonya did *not* want to meet Drake's new girl, so she searched for a spot near the exit.

All the seats were full, and she had to slip out fast if Sheriff Anderson came in, so she took a spot against the back wall as the lights went out.

Beside her, something tugged her elbow.

"Zain! You scared me."

"Glad you made it." His teeth glistened in the projector light.

Did that grin mean Drake had told him about Toronto?

Before she could find out the film started, opening on Grand Island. It was night, and Zain marched past the camera wearing an elf costume. When he knocked on the door to Betty's shack, the door fell, raising a puff of dust.

The audience laughed, and Drake whispered to his new girl, "That's our Buster Keaton moment." Sometimes Tonya hated having dragon hearing.

Onscreen, Grace and Zain crept into Betty's shack. The shots alternated between close-ups of their faces as they explored the ramshackle interior. Tonya had seen it from the outside many times, and she appreciated the atmospheric lighting the Ninjas had used to make it creepy.

Spooky sounds drew Grace outside and behind the building where Zain kicked a pile of fallen leaves. Grace crouched to clear them away, revealing white bones in the moonlight.

Zain picked up a long curved bone and pretended it was a bow, then grabbed a straight bone and pulled it back as if shooting an arrow. "Kapow!"

The camera cut to Grace, who glared. "Have some respect. That's a dead creature."

"Oooo, what kind? Are you missing any cute little bunnies?"

"Not funny."

Zain looked at the bone in his hand, shuddered, and dropped it to hoots and applause from the audience. His teeth chattered. "I d-d-don't think they *are* animal bones."

"Stop playing games." Grace kicked the leaves aside until a human skull rolled out of the pile. After a beat, she said, "Call the police."

Zain's hands shook as he tried to dial, then he held the phone up for Grace to see. "No bars. There's no service on this island."

"Let's go back to the boat." Grace led the way through the trees.

The rest of the movie showed them trying and failing to leave the island as angry ghosts, possessed animals, and poltergeists threw everything they had at them—literally. After a lengthy pursuit through the trees, one vengeful ghost forced Zain onto the pier and knocked him into the water. Dressed in a white suit, Arjun played the softly glowing phantom. With superhuman strength, the ghost thrust Zain's head underwater and held him until he ceased to struggle.

With everything she'd been through recently, the effect was a little too realistic for Tonya, but the story wasn't over yet.

Under a full moon, Grace retreated to the top of the round granite hill on Grand Island. She stared at the water where Zain had perished and prayed for the sun to rise before a ring of angry ghosts reached her from below.

Fade to black.

Wolf whistles and applause greeted the credits, and when the lights came on, Grace, Zain, and Arjun bowed to a standing ovation. Tonya clapped until her hands stung, then went to shake Zain's hand. He pulled her into a bear hug.

"Congratulations!" she said. "That was fantastic." Except there was something hinky about the skeleton they unearthed. "Where did you get the bones?"

"A huge bear must've died on the island," Zain said. "It saved us buying a plastic skeleton, but it was my inspiration to add the rolling skull."

"They weren't bear bones. They came from a dragon." Her heart fluttered. "Is the skeleton still where you found it? Can you bring me to see the bones?"

Tonya had killed the male dragon that once lived with its mate, Flores. It was breathing fire at her friends at the time, so she hadn't worried about the carcass. It made sense that scavengers would eat the flesh off the skeleton, and it had been hidden under fall leaves.

But the flaw she noticed didn't make sense.

In the film, the bones looked white and clean, meaning scavengers had eaten the flesh. But the remains were fresh enough that the joints still held, resulting in a complete skeleton—minus the front claws. It was a clue that turned Tonya's previous assumptions upside down.

Donna wasn't murdered by a dragon, but somebody using the missing claws to make it look that way.

38

After the film, Tonya stayed long enough to congratulate Grace and say hello to Priya before the girls left for the holidays. Drake gave her an awkward wave, but they didn't speak. Tonya was grateful. What could she say after the incident in Toronto? The worst part of it was losing Drake to a new girl.

She would miss her friends over Christmas, but next fall would be worse. She'd lost an academic year recovering from her fight against Jack Waldock. In her final year, when her Toronto friends graduated and moved home from Loon Lake, she could still expect to run into Marta.

Her ex-bully had pestered Tonya with texts during the movie. When the last Digital Ninja left, she drifted up to the Hub Pub and called Marta. "What do you want?"

"I know who killed Donna. Meet me at the Hub Pub."

"It's too crowded. I'm coming to your place." Before Marta could object, she hung up.

Tonya had to leave after texting Sheriff Anderson a picture of the dragon skeleton minus the claws, which she took during the screening. If he believed her theory, that the murderer used claws to frame a dragon, the sheriff would back off Tonya and start looking for the real killer. If he didn't believe her, he could deduce her location from her photo of the movie screen and arrest her in the Ninja's clubhouse.

In the crisp night air, Tonya walked from campus to the Ashton family compound, giving her time to wonder. Why would Marta ask for help? Her brother Stephen was deadly with a spell, and Marvin dressed like a dweeb but was ruthless and strategic with money. Between them, Tonya didn't think an enemy existed that they couldn't flatten or buy out. Was it Marta's suspicion of her uncles that led her to Tonya, or was it the Ashton family's distrust of authority that made her bypass National and seek Tonya's help?

Little did Marta know Tonya had to cover every angle in order to clear her name.

Marta was waiting out front. Maybe she had guessed how badly Tonya wanted an excuse to go inside and search the mansion for clues. Seeing an incomplete dragon skeleton in the movie had revolutionized her perspective. The murderer could have killed the mayor using the missing dragon's claws to frame someone. There was a very short list of people that National would suspect, like Helen, Roberto, and Paloma Alvarez—all enemies or rivals of the Ashton family.

"My dad's lawyer sent us a registered letter. They're going to contest the will." Martha didn't invite Tonya in.

"I thought he didn't have a hope."

Marta whispered, "We should go for a walk."

Through the December chill, Marta led Tonya around the back of the mansion and through the gardens. Dramatic lighting revealed topiary shrubs shaped like forest animals. Close to the house, rabbits and deer surrounded pots of purple and green ornamental cabbages. As she approached the fancy iron gate at the far end, spotlights gave crouching panthers and a proud lion an aura of evergreen strength. Marta brushed off Tonya's questions until they passed through the gate and crossed the road onto a neighboring farmer's property.

Loon Lake City was a bustling university town, but patches of farmland held out against the suburban sprawl. Grabbing her hand, Marta hurried Tonya through the cornfield to an enormous chestnut tree.

"You need to prove my suspicions before I tell anybody."

"What?"

"My father killed Mom to get her money, and he doesn't care about the law. Dad intimidated Mom's accountant until he blabbed the password, then drained her bank account. Uncle Marvin is fighting with the bank to get the money back. Dad's lawyer claims incorporation can't protect assets that belonged to him before."

"The family estate?"

"You mean Grandpa's shack beside the municipal dump? My brothers decontaminated the land and built a mansion around the original kitchen. All Dad did was live in it for a short while." Hurt flashed in Marta's eyes.

She knew the feeling. As a teen, Helen had dumped baby Tonya on her sister Barbara and fled Loon Lake. "I'm so sorry."

"Dad murdered Mom."

"You have a right to be angry, but he couldn't have committed the murder."

"When she was alive, Mom protected us. Now he's back."

"Where's your dad's motive? According to your lawyer, his challenge won't work."

"I know he did it. Find the proof."

"Let me search the house for evidence."

"No." Marta glanced at the house. "If Stephen catches you nosing around, he'll kill you."

"Why Marta, I never knew you cared."

"Shut up. Use your brain to figure this out."

It didn't take dragon senses to smell Marta's desperation. "Let me in or no deal."

Marta smuggled Tonya in through the maid's entrance. Opening her dragon senses, Tonya sniffed every elegant dining room, living room, study, and parlor for traces of dragon claws. Find the dragon claws to find the murderer.

After an exhaustive search of the second floor, Tonya knew too much about Stephen's expensive taste in sports clothes and Marvin's tech fetish. His home office had a desk with four wide computer screens on it opened to spreadsheets.

Marta said Marvin wasted his life playing games, but it looked like he wasted it crunching numbers.

"You don't need to search my room," Marta objected, but Tonya gleefully invaded the domain of her former nemesis.

In a closet big as a bedroom, she discovered outfits with jewelry that Marta had assembled on hangers—many with the price tags still attached. In her own way, Marta was as spoiled as her brother Stephen.

Marta stood by, air-washing her hands, unable to stop Tonya from snooping through her shoes, lingerie drawer, and jewelry boxes. Tonya lifted the mattress unnecessarily to peek underneath. Her dragon senses were powerful enough to sniff the claws through a closed drawer, but this was a fraction of payback for that time Marta laughed while her mean-girl friends flushed Tonya's purse in the toilet.

The rec room was stocked with grown up toys, and the cellars held sports equipment and wine racks. The kitchen was modern, polished, and completely devoid of skeletal remains.

"I'll check outside now."

Marta trailed her, looking over her shoulder as Tonya crisscrossed the grounds, sniffing quietly so Marta wouldn't guess at her new powers.

Tonya ran out of places to search. "There's nothing here. Your dad is innocent." And unfortunately, so were Marta's brothers. "Let me know if you find a real clue."

"How? My uncles watch everything I do. Marvin thinks I'm depressed and won't leave me alone."

"Let me handle it." Tonya wanted justice for Marta. Her ex-bully had suffered enough and wouldn't heal until she had closure. "I won't stop looking until I find out who did this to you."

Assuming she could evade Sheriff Anderson.

39

Tonya wove between tourists on her way to Loon Lake Village. At the wall, an Ashton guard nodded her through the broad stone archway, and she emerged into pandemonium.

Immediately she was bulldozed into a wall beside the archway by a handful of shouting tourists. Stumbling to the side, she stepped in rainbow goop, the byproduct of random spell-slinging. Little blobs of it littered the streets. Tonya went to rub it off in the grass, and smoke rose from her winter boots as the rubber soles melted. Watching her step, she fled down a cobblestone side street. It was quieter there among the century-old houses and mature trees, but the back of Tonya's neck prickled. Was somebody following her? She sniffed the air, but scents of corn dogs, popcorn, and funnel cakes from roadside carts overwhelmed her nose.

At a cart selling sunglasses, she pretended to admire a pair of mirror shades using the reflection to sneak a peek behind her. Nobody looked suspicious, but it was hard to tell. Any of these tourists could be spying on her, but they couldn't stop her from trying to figure out who would have wanted to frame Helen, Tonya, Roberto, or Paloma.

Tonya's first stop was the Alvarez's Condor Bakery. The scent of bread and golden empanadas in the glass case made Tonya's mouth water. She purchased a pastry from the lone teen behind the counter, but he couldn't tell her where to find Roberto or his parents.

Next, she tried the building site where contractors were adding new stories onto the historic Loon Lake Hotel, now owned by the Alvarez's. Table saws screamed as workers clad in protective gear bustled about, moving tools and supplies. If the family wasn't at work or supervising the renovations, Tonya would try their home. After the way Paloma had drugged her for interrogation, it would be a pleasure to invade Paloma's privacy and ask uncomfortable questions.

The prickling sensation on the back of her neck increased. Over her shoulder, Tonya spotted Sheriff Anderson. She left the charming commercial street and ventured down a maze of side streets until she finally reached the grand entrance to the Alvarez family's stately home guarded by ornate wrought-iron gates.

She buzzed the intercom and a tinny voice on the other end asked for her name. The gates unlocked with a satisfying click, and she walked up a long drive, the sound of her footsteps crunching against the pristine white gravel. Recently settled in Loon Lake, the Alvarez family had already improved the property with tennis courts, a two-story parking garage, and an artificial stream with a stone bridge and koi pond.

Paloma Alvarez opened the door herself. "I can see you soon."

She invited Tonya to sit in an exquisitely furnished drawing room crowded with curiosity cabinets, framed paintings, and antique furniture. How she had accumulated so many old things in such a short time was a mystery, but the bigger surprise was Anderson sitting on a horsehair sofa sipping tea.

Tonya retreated, but he called her back. "Truce? I promise not to arrest you here."

"Why?"

"Neutral ground. Paloma won't tell National you were here."

"Does this mean you don't suspect me?"

"To forgive that bully Marta, then offer to help her, isn't something a murderer would do."

"How do you..."

"For years I've heard about your life from Helen."

"What does she do for you?"

He rubbed his chin. "She watches over Loon Lake Village. This town used to escape notice by not using magic, but it has tremendous reserves of power. National needed someone to prevent evil influences from infiltrating."

"You mean like Jack Waldock?"

"National doesn't settle local disputes, but it tries to protect the powerless."

A servant with a white apron brought Tonya a cup of tea.

When she was out of earshot, Anderson continued. "Now that Loon Lake has joined the larger magical world, National doesn't need secret reports. Helen can retire."

Tonya moved closer and lowered her voice. "Do you think Paloma killed Donna?"

He shrugged. "Without opposition, the Alvarez family can redevelop Loon Lake Village however they like."

"Their dragon, Flores, could have been the murder weapon," Tonya agreed. "Or somebody might be framing them." She explained the claw theory to Anderson.

"So, according to you, whoever smells of dragon carcass is the murderer?"

Or who smelled of the minty cologne she'd detected on the body—which included Helen and Anderson. "Lots of people disagreed with Donna's policies or disliked her family, but few can control a dragon. Can Paloma?"

At that moment, Senora Alvarez swanned into the room wearing an elegant white dress. Without the lace shawl draped around her, Paloma looked younger with a muscular figure Tonya hadn't noticed before.

Paloma took a straight-backed chair facing the sofa. Her hands were dry and flaky, as if she had been scrubbing them. Whatever the chemical, it worked. Even when she passed a plate of cookies, Tonya couldn't detect a whiff of dragon on her.

Paloma smiled. "Tonya, I never expected a visit from you."

She matched Paloma's light tone. "I can't resist doing a good deed, and it's possible someone is trying to frame you. Are you capable of controlling a dragon?"

"Roberto tries with his rats and his whistle. My interest in dragons is more biological."

Tonya flinched under her avid gaze.

Anderson pushed his cup and saucer aside and set a folder on the table, spreading the photos for Paloma to see. "Can you tell what kind of dragon did this?"

Paloma picked up one photo, set it down, then spread the rest on the table. "The crime feels personal in a human way. The body is deeply scored, but nothing was eaten, not even the guts. A dragon would have at least tasted the liver."

"Are you sure?" Anderson gathered up the pics.

"It could have been a shifter."

"Now that I've tried to prevent someone from framing you," Tonya glared at Paloma, "this is your chance to apologize for kidnapping me."

"I'm very, very sorry," she said sarcastically before turning to the sheriff. "Can I keep her overnight next time? There are some tests National would have to sanction. Imagine, if we learned her secret, we could raise an army of dragon people."

Smiling, Anderson put a hand on her forearm and looked her in the eyes. "You've done enough. In fact, your experiments on this young woman broke so much ground that I've told dragon shifters all over the world about them." He pulled her closer. "I bet some of them are eager to congratulate you in person."

She blanched and pulled away, hugging herself as if sheltering her arms under the missing shawl. "What do you want?"

Speaking softly, Anderson towered over Paloma. "This is a courtesy visit, so I can eliminate your family from the investigation. Where were you on the night Mayor Ashton was killed?"

"We ate a family dinner here and then watched a movie in our home cinema."

"What about Roberto?" Tonya asked. "He stays on the island with Flores."

"Not that night." Paloma smiled sweetly. "Ask the housekeeper; she'll swear to it."

"Thank you." Anderson nodded as if satisfied with Roberto's alibi. "We'll keep in touch."

Paloma lifted her chin to look Anderson in the eye. "I have a question for National."

"Yes?"

"When are they going to release the cruise ship? My clients feel trapped, and some are threatening legal action."

"We apologize for any inconvenience, but National can't release the ship until we have found the perpetrator."

"In that case, you'd better get to work."

Wait, I have questions too.

Ask anything you like, Hatch. Since their psychedelic volcano experience, Tonya and Hatch were on speaking terms—not exactly buddies—but he had rescued her from complete humiliation in Toronto.

My question is for Bjorn.

Trust Hatch to be on a first-name basis with the sheriff.

Not here, Anderson replied.

Did he think Paloma could listen telepathically? Tonya waited until they reached the street to tell Anderson what she was thinking. "I searched the Ashton family compound with Marta, but the claws weren't there. I need to talk to Roberto on the island."

And I want to meet my mother, Flores, but I'm trapped inside Tonya. How do I talk to her?

Anderson reached for Tonya's shoulder but thought better of it. *I'd transform first and approach with caution, Hatch. Flores isn't a shifter like me or a hybrid like you. She's 100 percent dragon, a wild animal.*

But intelligent? Can she talk?

You'll see.

"Perfect." Tonya wouldn't relent until she examined the missing bones herself. "You can search the cruise ship for the missing dragon claws while I speak to Roberto. Drop me at the island when you go?"

We could fly there, Hatch proposed.

"I'll feel safer with Roberto if he knows the sheriff is my ride home."

40

Remembering how the inspector from National had stepped into the courtroom out of thin air at Helen's trial, and the sudden appearance of the red pavilion portal into National's police station, Tonya asked Sheriff Anderson, "Can we use instant travel to get to Grand Island?"

"That's not a good idea."

"Why?"

"This town had a good thing going. You gathered magical energies leaking into this dimension through ley lines, and you had a whole ancestor magic thing that's practically unique."

"Isn't that how everybody uses magic?"

"You can't run an international multidimensional organization like National messing about with old bones and ley lines." He lowered his voice. "We get our magic from the Other World."

This was a new concept for Tonya. She knew there was the world and the universe, of course. "You mean alien planets?"

"My dear sweet summer court child, this whole town is so naïve. Your ancestors figured out a way to get magic without paying the price, and because—up til now—you've been so small-time, the Others haven't bothered to make you pay for it."

"Others?"

"I'm not afraid to say it. Fairies." His big shoulders hunched as if he could wrap them around a secret. "They give us the immense power to travel anywhere on the globe in an instant by making a tiny detour through Fairyland. In exchange, my organization has to deal with the Fair Folk, which you do not."

"Fairyland? Like Peter Pan and Narnia?"

"The Fairy Realm. It's as real as our world but not nearly as pleasant. And Tonya," he lifted his hand like he wanted to touch her face but settled for stroking his chin, "if they ever hear about a one-of-a-kind accidental dragon-witch hybrid like you ... they won't rest until they capture you and bring you back to the Winter Queen who adores dissecting creatures to see how they work."

Tonya shivered. Of course she'd heard folktales, but Anderson confirmed elves existed. What had Donna done when she opened up Loon Lake to the greater mystical world?

"Boat rental, then?" It was December, but if Anderson went to the owner's house ...

"Nah, let's borrow a police boat." A grin lit up his face.

"You love your job, don't you?"

It was easy for Anderson. Out of thin air he stepped onto a police boat at the police dock and drove it away. A touch of magic ensured that everyone was looking the other way, that lenses on the security cameras fogged up, and chainsaws in the forest covered the engine roar.

Fifteen minutes later, Tonya joined him at a private dock. The motor rumbled, and Tonya shouted in Anderson's ear, "I don't understand why we're searching the ship! It's massive, and if a tourist murdered Donna, they could have thrown the murder weapon in the lake or dumped it in town!"

"Magic leaves traces," he yelled over the engine, "and I have the perfect tool to find them!"

As they skimmed over the water, spray misted Tonya's face and sunshine dazzled in a pale blue sky. This was a fine way to travel. She'd dressed for it in winter gloves, a hat, boots, and a coat, which was perfect until they pulled alongside the cruise ship. The air suddenly heated to summer temperatures. What had they done? Bottled the Bahamas and carried the weather with them?

She pulled off her hat, mitts, and coat with one eye on the cruise ship rising and falling on the waves. "Aren't you worried they'll run us over?"

A pair of National officers opened a door ten feet above the waterline and rolled out a pilot's ladder.

"Stay here. I'll drive you to the island once we've searched the ship." He started climbing the ladder, but Tonya clambered on behind him, trying not to swing the ladder too much as she rose.

"What are you doing?"

"I'm coming with you. There's no way I want the police to catch me sitting in their boat."

The sheriff opened his mouth to argue, thought better of it and kept climbing.

If there was something onboard National didn't want her to see, Tonya was determined to see it. How far did she trust National, anyway? They dealt with elves, which was bad apparently. They ruled without mercy or care for local issues. For all she knew, they would do a superficial search for the bones, and she'd never know for sure whether a tourist had killed Donna. Or an assassin had arrived by ship to do the job.

On deck, Tonya recognized the turtle detective from the police station. A couple of burly officers could be bodybuilders or werewolves. A prickle at the back of her neck made her turn. She faced the sexy vampire detective from the other day and her Amazonian partner in leather armor. Both of them carried crates labeled "fragile."

Officers and detectives grouped around Anderson as they prepared to search for traces of dragon bones and claws in particular.

Tonya scanned the sky, nervous that Flores might come to investigate the commotion and spot her. When she didn't fly over, Tonya decided that National could take all the time they wanted searching the ship, because she was in no hurry to interview Roberto on the island. After killing the dragon's mate, Tonya assumed Flores would want revenge.

On the top deck, Anderson gathered the officers and instructed them to search every cabin, closet, and container for the missing dragon claws.

"Searching the ship will take us all day," a burly werewolf objected. "I have my own cases."

"Not a problem." The vampire kneeled to open a crate, giving everyone a view of her cleavage. She handed jars to her partner, who distributed them among the officers. Each jar held a glowing fluffy gray moth.

"These are coffin-nosed moths," the warrior woman explained. "Spread yourselves through the ship and open your jars. They'll sniff out anything that has come in contact with the remains of a magical creature."

The werewolf looked relieved. "So, we don't have to go door-to-door?"

"Search every cabin, engine room, and cargo hold right down to the brig," Anderson said. "We're only doing this once."

"What about the tourists?" the werewolf asked.

"Send them back to their cabins. They can watch us search, so they can't claim we stole anything. Runnymede?"

The turtle detective moseyed over to Anderson. "Yeah?"

"You're in charge of liaison. Find the captain and explain how National operates."

The turtle man stood on his hind legs and grinned, deepening every wrinkle in his ancient face. "It will be my pleasure."

The procedure was simple, but the ship was huge. The length of two football fields and fifteen stories high, there were over six hundred cabins to search. Tourists who hadn't gone ashore clustered in one of six bars, three restaurants, the spa, the pool, or casino. They grumbled quietly when the cruise director got on the P.A. system and ordered them back to their cabins, but nobody dared oppose the fearsome powers of National.

The door-to-door search of the cabins, facilities, and the mechanical rooms below decks looked like it would take many hours. As the detectives and officers started, the captain, a short man covered in dark woolly hair, came after Anderson, waving his fists. Runnymede followed, puffing after him.

Red in the face, the captain ranted in an accent Tonya didn't recognize. "Let my ship go! You make me lose a quarter million a day!"

Runnymede placed himself between the captain and Anderson. "You want me to lay it out, boss?"

It was late afternoon by the time Tonya clambered back aboard the OPP boat. It felt extra cold after spending the morning in the cruise ship's tropical bubble. Anderson opened the throttle, sending the twenty-foot craft climbing and dropping over the icy waves. The freezing spray numbed Tonya's feet and hands. By the time they reached the Grand Island pier, ice stiffened the ends of her hair and she shivered.

Pitiful human, so whiny and weak. We could have flown and been back by now.

Make yourself useful and heat us from the inside, she retorted.

Hand over control to me, and you'll never feel cold again.

Nope, we're working together from now on. She'd make sure of it.

If Anderson overheard the exchange, he didn't comment. As he pulled alongside the pier, Tonya leaped out and helped tie up. They had already discussed where Zain and Grace found the bones filmed in the Ninja's movie, so Anderson knew where to look.

He strode along the beach to the shack and located a shovel in a nearby shed where Tonya found an antique rake. Anderson turned over leaves and dirt near the shack, checking for the dragon claws. Tonya helped with one eye on the sky, watching for Flores.

She redoubled her efforts. The sooner she found the bones, the sooner she could leave the place where she'd killed the dragon's mate. "I'm sure this is the spot where I saw the bones in the movie. Why aren't they here?"

"Wait."

He pulled a jar out of each pocket and released a couple of glowing coffin-nosed moths. They fluttered to a pile of leaves ten feet away. Instead of remaining on the surface, they disappeared into the leaves. Tonya didn't see them again until Anderson borrowed her rake to sweep away the leaf litter.

Up close, she watched the little critters sucking something out of the bones through tiny black proboscises, the way butterflies suck nectar.

When they seemed sated, Anderson coaxed the moths back into the jars. They clung to the sides, slowly opening and closing their glowing wings.

"What are they eating?" The bones looked clean.

"The moths feed off the death energy of magical creatures." It was the same principle the Old Families used to capture the power of dead practitioners in the cemetery.

When Anderson turned his back, she crouched to sniff the ground for traces of the minty scent she'd found at the beach. Nothing.

She stood up quickly when he faced her. "You were right," he said. "Somebody took the front claws but left the rest of the bones."

"Will you bring in a forensics team to look for more clues?"

"Not necessary. Whoever did this wore gloves and protective clothing. I don't smell anything, and the moths turn black when they taste death magic, so no sign of necromancy."

"If you let them free, could the moths lead us to whoever did this?" she asked.

"They don't work at a distance. What about Betty? I've been researching the local lore, and she's supposed to live on a hill overlooking the beach. Maybe she saw whoever took the claws."

"Your info is out of date," Tonya replied. "She moved away. We should talk to Roberto."

"Are you sure you don't want to wait in the boat?"

"I'm not afraid of Flores."

Liar. Hatch laughed and Anderson must have heard it but didn't comment.

He strode back to the beach and along the sand to the enormous pavilion, where Roberto trained Flores. Stopping in front of a human-sized tent flap, Anderson called, "Roberto! It's Sheriff Anderson."

Roberto drew aside the flap, blinking in the winter sunlight. When he ushered them in, Tonya noticed scorch marks on the ceiling, and an unmade camp bed near a temporary kitchen counter and sink. Despite subzero temperatures outside, the heat indoors made her remove her hat and unzip her coat.

"Mom told me to expect you." Roberto stared at Tonya.

"I need to ask some questions." Anderson kept his voice soft. "We're hoping you might have seen something to help with our inquiries into Donna's death."

"There's no point. I was on the island with Flores when Donna died."

"Alone?" Anderson didn't mention Paloma's family movie night alibi.

"If Flores was flying, someone would have seen her."

"So far no one's come forward." Anderson pulled a large evidence bag from his pocket. "I need a DNA sample from Flores."

"A cheek swab? Getting that'll be fun." Roberto's eyes twinkled.

"A cast-off scale will do." He toed the ground with his shoe. "She's probably dropped one somewhere around here." Anderson held out the bag while Roberto searched the sandy floor of the pavilion.

When Roberto found an opalescent scale, Anderson called out, "Wait. Let me use gloves."

"Are we finished?" Roberto held open the tent flap, but Anderson stood his ground.

"Call Flores. I want to examine her."

"This time of day she's usually fishing."

"If she doesn't follow your orders, you must stop claiming she improves local security." Anderson crossed his arms, his legs a sturdy A-frame built to outlast the protests of any witness. "Call her."

With a shrug, Roberto threw on a coat and walked the shore, his hair whipping in the wind. He put a silver whistle to his lips and blew.

Even from inside the tent, the high-pitched sound hurt Tonya's ears.

How annoying! Hatch complained. *Imagine having an annoying sound in your head telling you where to go.*

Yeah, just imagine. Through the tent flap, Tonya scanned the horizon for Flores.

Coward, Hatch chuckled.

When the dragon didn't appear immediately, Roberto whistled again and again, hurting Tonya's sensitive ears.

He came back inside the pavilion. "Looks like she's busy."

"Or she doesn't obey you." Tonya frowned. Helen could influence Flores. She'd stopped the dragon from attacking Tonya when it was angry. By contrast, Roberto couldn't get her to come for a treat. "You use a whistle to train Flores. It's not exactly mind control, is it?"

"You would know."

"I'm disappointed you couldn't get her," Tonya lied. The dragon had laid an egg inside her, and Tonya had killed the dragon's mate. Each had hurt the other in unforgivable ways.

Anderson dug his feet into the sand. "We can wait til she comes back."

"Fine." Roberto opened a bin and snatched up a reeking cloth bag that squeaked and wriggled in his hand. This time, when he went outside to blow his whistle, he held up the bag.

In minutes, Tonya spotted a speck growing on the horizon as Flores skimmed over the lake. Roberto waited until she was close, then threw a rat into the air. She caught it on the fly and, when Roberto gave two sharp blasts of his whistle, she banked sharply and landed on the sand.

"Querida Mamacita." Roberto fed her rats by the wriggling handful until she lay on her back and let him scratch under her chin with a plastic ice scraper. The joy of getting a good scratch made her wriggle on the sand with her eyes closed, her tail wagging with pleasure.

When the scratching paused, she opened her eyes, spotted Tonya, and leaped to her feet blasting a plume of fire which Tonya barely dodged.

"Control your animal or I'll shoot!" Anderson aimed a pistol between the beast's eyes.

Flores froze, smart enough to recognize a gun. She backed away, dropping her head to the sand in a subservient gesture.

When Anderson lowered his weapon, Roberto patted her muzzle and shushed her. "Naughty Flores. We don't breathe fire at guests."

The dragon's tail thrashed like an angry cat's. "Lie down, Flores." He stared her down until she looked away. Reluctantly, she lowered her massive snout to the sand and stretched her paws in front of her.

"Make sure she doesn't move." Still wearing gloves, Anderson examined her body until he found a whitish scale sticking out at an odd angle. It was coming off, so she didn't react when he plucked it and put it in an evidence bag.

When that was done, he walked in front of her snout and looked her in the eye. *Did you kill Mayor Donna Ashton?*

Tonya heard his telepathic question, but no telepathic answer from Flores.

Putting his hands on either side of the dragon's snout, Anderson pictured Donna in his mind, allowing Tonya to see it too.

There was a flicker of recognition on Flores's face, and she responded in kind. Tonya saw the image of Donna standing atop the boat rental building. Red and white bunting adorned the balcony. Flores remembered seeing Donna the day she gave her victory speech. She also remembered scattering the crowds and strafing the beach with blasts of flame.

That's not what we're here to talk about, Anderson insisted. *I need to know if you killed this woman or if you saw who did.*

This woman. Guilty. Flores pointed a claw at Tonya.

41

With a roar, Flores released a stream of fire. Sprinting away, Tonya darted this way and that until Flores trapped her against the shore. She tried to go left, but the dragon blocked her escape with unfurled wings. There was no way past the dragon, so before Flores could roast her alive, Tonya splashed into the frigid water and dove.

The cold knocked the air from her lungs, and her limbs clenched in the frigid water. She was a strong swimmer, but every time she swam for shore Flores intercepted her. A rim of ice had formed near the beach, proving the water too cold to survive. At most, she had a few minutes before hypothermia took her. As her body temperature dropped, her muscles stiffened and her movements slowed and she fought against drowsiness, struggling to stay conscious.

Water closed over her head and Tonya thrashed, or at least she tried to. Her arms and legs refused to respond, and she yearned to sleep. It was good to close her eyes. The pain of the cold faded, like when your hands ache on a frigid day and then stop hurting because the blood has left them.

She was dying and dreaming, and she didn't want to die, did she? Hatch wouldn't want to die.

Hatch?

He was mesmerized staring at Flores, his mother, but she knew how it felt to be Hatch now. In Toronto, she'd been fully conscious and willing when he triggered the transformation. All it took was the will to begin, the cracking of bones and a fire in the belly.

Fire.

And warmth enough to save her from the frigid water.

Bring on the change.

It started, strangely painless in her hypothermic state, but hurt more as bones broke and reformed—and blood heated.

Born to swim, even in this unfamiliar form, she became Hatch/Tonya flapping her wings to fly underwater, stabilized like a torpedo by her powerful tail. She surfaced for an overdue breath, filling her immense lungs, protected from the cold by her thick scales.

She'd transformed and survived. Fat lot of good Anderson had done. Wasn't he supposed to protect her? He should have shifted into dragon form and fished her out of the water by now. Something was wrong.

Raising her head, she peered at the tent and wished the flap was open so she could see what was happening. Meanwhile, Flores leaped into the sky and flew for Loon Lake City. Good riddance!

Watch out! Hatch's voice warned in her head.

Why? Shouldn't Flores leave her alone now that she had turned into Hatch?

It wasn't until Flores banked and turned, diving at Tonya, that she understood. Flores didn't recognize her child. She saw a strange dragon or a dragon that was Tonya. Either way, Flores was about to attack.

With a flick of her tail, Tonya sprinted for the bottom of the lake, desperate to go deep before Flores crashed onto her.

Too slow.

Flores smashed onto Tonya's back, knocking the wind out of her and making her gasp and swallow water. Gripped in the larger dragon's front claws, Tonya wasn't ready when Flores rolled her over and kicked her in the belly. Tonya wrenched her body aside before Flores's toe claws slammed into empty water. If Flores had connected, the claws would have sliced open Tonya's abdomen.

Breaching to take a breath of air, Tonya looked to shore, but Roberto wasn't calling off his dragon. The men hadn't emerged from the tent, so there would be no help from them. Flores flew too well to evade in the sky, but Tonya was a water baby. Her best chance for survival was the lake. She dove deep, looking for weeds or a deep spot to hide in.

There, close to the island, the water got deeper. The Ninjas had shot a movie using the hidden cave under the island. If Tonya needed a breath, she could swim through the underwater tunnel to the secret beach.

She dove into the deepest spot and stirred up the muck to decrease visibility, but it didn't work. Too soon Flores approached, circling and looking for an opening to attack.

What is your beef with me?

But in her heart, Tonya knew and regretted what she'd done. Saving the swimmers at the expense of baby dragons. There had been no choice and yet she felt guilty. She was guilty. Flores wouldn't rest until she punished Tonya, unless ...

Speak up, Hatch. Don't you want to meet your mother?

Either he was pouting or too scared to speak.

Hatch, say hello to your mother.

Mother?

The circling dragon pulled up short and looked down at Tonya through the murk and dove.

The dragons circled each other, warily closing in and retreating. Hatch called out telepathically. *Mom! Don't you recognize me? I'm your kid.*

Flores came at Tonya, but instead of attacking, she made an excited crooning noise while Tonya held still.

Mom, it's me.

Hatch crooned back, and that's when the fierce-looking dragon opened her mouth, extended a prehensile tongue, and licked Tonya's belly.

Baby?

Mommy! Hatch replied.

With a whoop of joy, Flores darted below Tonya and nosed her up to the surface where she swam in excited circles around her. They made a bubbly dragon-go-round together until Tonya got dizzy and wanted out of the water.

Tail swishing, she headed for the beach where Roberto staggered out of the tent clutching the side of his face. He had a black eye and blood dripped from a cut on his forehead. Anderson strode after him, his lip swollen and bleeding but otherwise unharmed.

Nice interrogation technique. In dragon form, Tonya trotted past them and nosed open the flap. Inside the enormous tent, in front of a small heater, she basked to dry her scales.

Let's go back outside! Hatch insisted. *I need to see my mother.*

Patience, Hatch. Unless you want her to eat us, she needs to know you're still inside me in human form.

Hatch didn't resist transformation. Shifting bones and shrinking huge wings and claws and scales lanced her with pain as they reabsorbed into her body. At least it went quickly, now that she knew the painful trick to trigger the change. To instantly access her humanity and revert to human, all Tonya had to do was picture Drake and break her heart again, remembering what she'd lost.

Tonya strode out of the pavilion wearing her long coat, boots, mitts, and not much else. Shifting was murder on her wardrobe.

The men lay panting on the beach, too tired to fight anymore. Flores lay on the sand beside Roberto, licking his wounds with her long tongue.

Anderson heaved himself to his feet. "Roberto didn't do it."

"Is that why you beat him up?" Tonya quipped.

"He started it." Anderson spit out sand. "We should go."

"Not yet." A question had been bothering Tonya since Flores recognized Hatch and stopped trying to kill her. "What is National going to do about Flores?"

His eyes widened. "You want to press charges?"

"Ashton Security uses Flores to keep people in check, and Roberto trains her with a whistle and feeds her rats like a snake."

Anderson didn't reply.

"She's an intelligent, magical being."

Roberto got up heavily. "And you killed her babies."

"Which I'll always regret but look at what this community is doing. They take this noble, intelligent animal and treat it like a slave. What is National going to do about that?"

42

At the public pier, Anderson walked Tonya to his vehicle, got a car blanket out of the back seat, and handed it to her. The soft fleece was comforting and took away her shivers.

"Get in." He blasted the heater, which came out cold as they pulled away from the beach. The car had warmed slightly by the time they reached campus. He pulled up to the curb outside the Mackenzie residence and walked her to the ground floor cafeteria.

Once Tonya was seated by the floor-to-ceiling window, he brought her a hot tea and stirred in three sugar packets. "Drink."

The first sip tasted like syrup. Making a face, she put it down.

"Finish the whole thing." He put his hands on her shoulders. "Not many people could survive that swim plus a tussle with Flores. National is very grateful for your help in the investigation, but I made a huge mistake bringing you."

Her lips felt stiff against the paper cup. "Don't cut me out of the investigation. I have connections. Did you know Donna spoke with a ghost on the beach the night she died?"

"We'll follow up."

"What about the dragon claws? Did you search for traces of them on Roberto?"

"The whole island smells of the dead dragon, because it lived there and marked its territory."

"Is that the same as skeletal claws? To my dragon senses, they smell like carrion, not cast-off scales."

"What you smell, I smell. There's no need to risk yourself anymore. If the killer thinks you know something, you could be next." He braced his hands on the table and locked eyes with her. "I'll send a team of officers canvassing for witnesses and going door-to-door with coffin-nosed moths. Leave it to us."

"What about Marta's father? He skipped the funeral but came back to town to claim Donna's property."

"He has an alibi. Now, rest up and relax. A few more minutes in the water and you would have died." He pushed back his chair.

Tonya touched his forearm. "What about an irate citizen or a City Counselor who wanted Donna out of the way?"

"There's no indication it was a Counselor, and National has been infiltrating the protests at City Hall. Using coffin-nosed moths, they've discovered plenty of magical contraband on the protesters but no trace of dragon claws."

"Only a powerful practitioner would dare kill Donna. Her brother, Stephen, can paralyze or kill you with disease." Tonya stared at the dissolved sugar clinging to the bottom of her cup. With the shivers gone, blood rushed back into her fingers and toes accompanied by throbbing pain.

"Is there someone I can call? You shouldn't be alone."

"I'd feel safer with you." And happier where the action was.

"If I don't solve the case soon, National Council will swoop in and either close it or make a quick judgment."

"Am I still the lead suspect?"

"Not in my opinion, but National…" He shrugged with open palms. "It's in your best interests to let me do my job."

"Will I see you again?"

"Let's hope not." He stood, gesturing for her to stay seated. "Call somebody to check on you. Get some rest and stay safe."

"Don't worry. I'll be fine."

"I see wheels turning behind that innocent expression. No more meddling in the case."

"You need insider help."

"We have Ashton Security and local cops charmed to work for us and forget about it afterward."

"Without me, you never would have known about those claws."

"Which we appreciate."

After the pain she'd suffered, Tonya had earned her place in the investigation. "Every tourist knew about Flores from the brochure. A witch hunter or an assassin could frame the dragon knowing National would eventually close the case."

"They'd never escape. The ship is spelled to stay in place until the investigation is over, and every being on the ship agreed to a tag charm that stops them from getting lost or going AWOL."

Tonya wasn't convinced. "If somebody's hunting powerful witches, Helen's next."

"Then stop arguing and phone your mother, so I can do my job. The pair of you would be safer together."

He was right. Tonya texted.

No reply.

She called and blood rushed to her cheeks, the blanket around her shoulders suddenly too warm. No response. Outsiders could kidnap Helen and force her to use her powers on animals. They could fix horse races, make hits look like random animal attacks, run undetectable, untraceable surveillance ... organized crime would love her.

"Please, can we drive to the Herbal Healing Shop?"

He nodded, and Tonya matched Anderson stride for stride to the car.

"She probably put the phone down without disconnecting." He threw himself behind the wheel.

"Helen didn't hear my telepathy when I was on the island fighting Flores. Did you?"

He reddened as they pulled away from the curb. "I heard you, but not Helen."

"Normally she can hear me from that distance. Do you think somebody figured out she was spying for National?"

"Doubt it." Anderson kept his eyes on the road. "She's been doing it for seventeen years."

Meaning since Tonya was tiny. "Or one of Donna Ashton's fanatical supporters might believe Helen manipulated an animal to kill her. Can't you drive faster?"

43

At the Herbal Healing Shop, Tonya raced to the back, through the door, and up Helen's stairs two at a time. She wasn't in the living room, so Tonya went up the stairs to the bedroom calling, "Helen! Helen!" Her telepathic shouts also went unanswered.

Anderson checked each room with military efficiency. "There's no sign of struggle."

Mom?

To Anderson she said, "Try telepathy."

Helen? Can you hear me?

Tonya covered her ears.

"Too loud?" he asked.

"Like an air horn in my head."

He took out his phone. "I'm sending the Mundane police a request to watch for Helen. Go back to the dorm and wait for one of us to call."

"Stop trying to send me to my room."

His expression softened. "If somebody is killing the most powerful witches in Loon Lake, you're next in line after Helen."

"Me, powerful?" She scoffed.

"You can transform into a dragon and kill by draining life energy."

"I'm not fully in control in dragon form."

"Yet."

"And I'd never kill anyone."

"Again."

"Settling Jack Waldock's revenant was *not* murder."

"Touchy. But I take your point. Stay with me until I can post a guard at your dorm."

"To keep me under house arrest?"

"For your protection."

"After you just called me a murderer?"

"I said come with me. Stop arguing after you've won."

They crossed Main Street and took a few quick turns, then drove through the gate into Loon Lake Village. Tonya would never get used to heavy traffic on her hometown's antique streets. Cars sat in a long, sluggish line as frustrated tourists leaped out and yelled or flung spells at each other. On the sidewalk, a visitor wearing a beer hat and Mardi Gras beads puked on the sidewalk while clusters of staggering merrymakers sang bawdy songs. They wore summer clothing spelled to repel the cold, but it looked weird to see people in shorts and flip-flops walk snow-dusted cobblestone streets.

Since the ship had been stuck in port, the vibrant atmosphere had soured, replaced by gangs of staggering tourists shouting and urinating on 200-year-old buildings. The local cops were busy somewhere else as a fistfight spilled out of a bar.

People banged on Anderson's car, so he rolled down his window.

"Release us. We're innocent!" they shouted. "You're from National. Help us leave."

A burly fellow with heavy gold chains and a nylon shirt bearing a flaming skull pushed to the front of the throng. "I shelled out plenty for this trip, and I've missed three ports of call." He punctuated his words by thumping the hood of the car. "Because I'm *marooned* in this *hopeless backwater village.*"

"There's an active homicide investigation." Anderson stepped out of the car to address the visitors. "The perpetrator targets practitioners, so you'd be safer on the ship."

As if in response, a slimeball spell exploded onto the windshield.

Skull shirt guy crowed, "That line didn't work on him any better than it worked on me."

Anderson cleared the window with a mystical gesture, then cast a bubble around the car to protect it. "Let's walk."

Complaining tourists trailed them for blocks, until, up ahead, Tonya saw her mother wearing a favorite blue blouse. She ran after her, shouting, "Helen! Wait!" but her mother turned down a narrow street in the oldest part of Loon Lake Village. Tonya followed her into an unpaved alley where well-to-do Victorians once kept coach houses now renovated into garages and workshops. Rushing to catch up, Tonya thought her mother looked tired, her shoulders curbed.

At last, the woman noticed Tonya and turned to face her. "Stop following me!"

She was the same height with long white hair, but it wasn't Helen.

"Sorry, my mistake." A hazard of living in a small city, people shopped at the same stores and bought the same clothes.

Back on the main street, Tonya and Anderson searched for Helen visually and telepathically in boutiques and restaurants until the sea of tourists nudged them down a side street. They circled the block until Anderson asked, "Why do I feel lost?"

"Sorry, that's the local merchants," Tonya explained. "They cast a browsing spell that makes you lose track of time and direction until you spend some money. Let me take care of it." She nipped into the Old-Time General Store to buy a pack of gum and reemerged in time to witness a strange sight.

In the street, a mother frantically rubbed at a rainbow of magical goop clinging to her writhing son's hands and t-shirt. The kid screamed, "Get it off me!"

Dropping the gum, Tonya raced to help.

Together, they pulled the squirming boy's shirt off his skinny frame, but the rainbow goop had sunk into his skin and steam rose where it made contact, breaking his magical protection against the elements. Icy wind tossed the boy's hair, and he shivered.

"You need to warm up." Tonya held out her hand, and the boy and his mother followed her into the store, where she purchased a bottle of water and a purse pack of Kleenex. The mother splashed her son's belly and cleaned off the residue with tissues.

"Thank you so much."

"Happy to help," Tonya said.

"Mom," the kid nagged. "Buy me nacho chips."

"It's almost lunch."

"Aw, Mom!"

When she held up a souvenir hoodie to keep him warm, he shook his head. "I'm too hungry to try things on."

Moments later, the boy grinned in the checkout line, stuffing his face and getting orange cheese on his new sweatshirt.

The mother touched Tonya's arm. "Let me pay you for the tissues and water."

"Don't bother. It's nothing."

"There must be some way to thank you."

"Well, there is one thing. May I?" She grabbed the kid's goopy shirt, wrapping it around itself to keep her coat pocket clean.

The street was a logjam of cars as Tonya and Anderson made their way back to the vehicle. Before they arrived, Tonya heard Helen's voice in her head.

People say you've been looking for me?

Helen was alive! *Where have you been?*

Trying to find out what Flores knows about the murder. Roberto called me and said you didn't have any luck questioning her.

Roberto is helping you?

He's keen to prove his family didn't do it.

What did Flores say?

Well, she's not chatty. Made me go fishing for hours before she opened up.

Fishing how?

I have SCUBA training.

I can't believe ... swimming with a dragon is too dangerous!

Anderson covered a smile. Evidently, he could hear their exchange.

Nonsense. I have the right gear, and a connection for heating spells. Flores showed me to a houseboat that sank in the 1950s—a real piece of history.

That's nice, but you should have told someone where you were going.

Yes, Mom. By the way, Flores doesn't know anything. She wasn't on the mainland when Donna died, and she didn't see anything useful, but I am absolutely diving near that sunken boat again. Want to come?

Anderson interrupted, "Helen's safe. I need to get back to work, and you can go home." He gestured at the car.

Tonya didn't get in. "I need to do something first. Meet me at the Ashton mansion in twenty minutes?" She itched to show him the shirt and explain what she wanted to do.

"Bad idea. After we questioned Ashton Senior and family, Stephen accused me of police harassment."

"So? He has a short fuse."

"I've already questioned the Ashtons, and it would antagonize Stephen to question them again without new evidence."

"I can."

"Don't put yourself in danger."

"So, you agree the Ashtons are prime suspects!"

"No, but you should leave this to the authorities."

"Relax. I'm just going to chat up an old school friend."

44

Tonya waved at the guard as she walked around the barrier and through the manicured gardens. Marta answered the door wearing black.

"What are you doing here?"

Her lips glistened crimson, and her perfect coif smelled of hairspray, reminding Tonya of Marta's mother. "I've cracked the case. Let me in?"

Marta frowned. "If you know something, shouldn't you be talking to National?"

"I couldn't wait."

Marta stepped back to let her in. "Don't expect me to pay you until my mother's murderer is behind bars."

"Of course." Tonya didn't expect Marta to pay her at all. She'd probably start insulting Tonya again once the crisis ended. "I figured out how it was done. A dragon didn't kill Donna. Somebody took the claws from a dragon skeleton and used them to murder your mother. I used to think somebody was trying to frame Helen, or the Alvarez family, but it was supposed to look like an accident so National wouldn't investigate."

"Who did it?"

"We'll know soon. Tomorrow morning, National will release magic-sniffing moths to search every cranny of Loon Lake. Once we find the claws and test them for magic traces, we'll know exactly who used them."

"Unless the murderer wore gloves."

"It won't matter," Tonya spoke earnestly. "Every practitioner has a signature, and every spell creates slimy waste that can be traced to the caster." She showed Marta the shirt covered in rainbow slime. "National can trace this mess to the tourist who made it. If the murderer so much as breathed on those claws, we'll know who did it."

"If you don't even have the claws," Marta wrinkled her nose, "why bother me?"

"We'll know soon, so I want you to be ready when I tell you who did it."

"So I'll have your cash on hand."

"Exactly." It was the only motive Marta would believe.

Marta smirked, mistaking Tonya for a sucker, but Tonya had outgrown high school drama. Of course, Marta would try to take advantage. Tonya hid her smile.

Marta's scorn would misdirect her from Tonya's real plan.

45

Tonya suspected what had occurred but couldn't prove it. For that, she would need Hatch's cooperation. Once again, she stood on the roof of the Mackenzie Residence.

I'd like to share the flight tonight. At least Hatch didn't call her a puny human. *I need your eyes and wings to fly over Loon Lake—without any barrel rolls or tricks.*

You got tired of passing out? He gave a soft chuckle. *What's in it for me?*

I've been unfair, Tonya admitted. *I've wasted opportunities fighting with you, because I felt like the victim.*

Go on. By his tone, Hatch was enjoying this. *Anything else you want to say to me?*

I'm sorry.

Apology not accepted. It's easy to say sorry when you want something.

Let me finish? I'm sorry for wanting to get rid of you. You're an intelligent being, and it was selfish of me to want free of you.

That doesn't reassure me you won't try to magic me away using the first evil wizard you can find.

There are evil wizards?

I don't know. I'm still a hatchling, remember? Ask me in a hundred years.

Wouldn't that be nice. *Please believe me. I'll never try to get rid of you again, and I'm willing to share our time from now on.*

Let me guess, you're offering me control on sick days and full moons.

No, but you have to let me go to classes and have a regular social life. Just not with Drake, because she'd pushed him away.

When am I in charge? Hatch asked. *How are we going to decide when there's a time conflict or you hate something I love?*

You mean like waking up with a stomach full of furry animals?

Yes, delicious furry animals. See what I mean? Hatch raised his voice in her head. *This won't work unless I make the rules.*

And we agree to break those rules in an emergency. Like now. If they didn't wind this up and get into the air, the murderer would get away. *How about we divide our time half and half, but you don't interfere with school and important social stuff?*

But I get to hunt for hairy animals?

Yes.

And you'll stop complaining all the time?

Sure.

And you'll buy me a trove of pretty things and a beautiful trunk to guard them in?

With a stainless-steel lock. Tonya owed him that much. *But I can't afford real gold, rubies, and emeralds. Without stealing, I promise to give you a pile of pretty things.*

The shinier the better?

Bring on the shiny. We can also visit your mother when you like—although Loon Lake would be safer if you convinced her to fly away.

She won't leave her cuddly boy 'til I'm grown, Hatch crooned. *She says I'm too adorable. But don't worry. In a hundred years, I'll be an adult and she'll be an empty nester, ready to travel the magical world.*

I'll be dead in a hundred years.

He chuckled. *Ignorant human. Together, we could live for centuries.*

Deal. So, let's fly but gently. I need to see the ground from the air without passing out.

Hatch groaned. *A dragon afraid of heights? You're like a bad joke.*

It's getting a bit better. On the way back from Toronto, when you flew over the clouds, it felt more like an airplane. I enjoy flying in planes.

You feel safer held up by a heavy metal tube than by your own wings? I'll never understand you, puny Tonya.

She didn't know whether to celebrate because he'd used her name or be offended by "puny." *Make sure I don't black out.*

Buckle up and put your seat in the upright position, Hatch said. *There may be some turbulence.*

Heat gathered in her belly and radiated out to her arms and legs. Tonya ditched her clothes in a pile and braced for the pain.

Breathe normally and relax, Hatch said. *I got this.*

The change threw her onto all fours as the bones inside her melted and re-formed, shifting to new positions. Her expanding body sent pain through every nerve, but the process went more smoothly when she wasn't fighting against it.

Minutes later, perched at the edge of the dormitory roof, Hatch reminded her, *You owe me a bellyful of rats for this.*

Yummy rats, got it—but first we're hunting humans.

Flying at low altitude might tempt a drunken tourist to cast spells at her, but she had to get close and see everything. They started over Loon Lake Village, making slow, wide circles that expanded to cover the city and the surrounding farmland and forest. She let Hatch taste the air for dragon scents and hints of decay, while she scanned the countryside for suspicious activity.

Well, that was nice. Time to bag me a fawn!

We haven't finished searching.

How long is this going to take?

Please, Hatch, I don't know, but I've set a trap. We're watching to see who takes the bait.

They searched for hours. Sometimes Hatch got distracted by vermin in the grass. A few times Tonya relented, and they grabbed a mousy bite on the wing, but she drew the line at baby deer. She was not eating Bambi!

Wings aching from the constant flapping and stomach distended from the rodents she'd eaten, Tonya could barely keep moving. The moon had set, and the trap had flopped. It was time to head home, clean the fur out of her claws, and admit defeat.

What do you say, Hatch? Bedtime?

Humans are so wimpy. If murder is as terrible as you say, we should fly until our wings fall off. Let's do one more circuit, starting from the center.

She hated to admit it, but he was right. One more go-round wouldn't kill her, especially if it forced Hatch to stop calling her puny. She'd prove humans were small but mighty.

Despite strained muscles, Tonya's eyelids were starting to droop when, flying over a fallow field, a silver flash caught her attention. Climbing above the clouds for cover, she spied two shadowy figures with shovels. At the center of the field, near the base of a scrubby birch, two men were digging a hole. Swooping closer on silent wings, she recognized Stephen and Marvin Ashton. The brothers were in it together!

She broadcast the news telepathically to Anderson, who promised to send his men for the arrest. Her shoulders ached, and Hatch whined in her ear, but nothing could dampen her elation when a cloudy ring surrounded the Ashton men. Detectives from National stepped out of the mist and clapped them into magic-retardant handcuffs.

Hatch roared in triumph. They had caught Mayor Ashton's killers.

High five Hatch!

Huh?

Tonya made a mental note not to high-five creatures with wings. *Let's go home.*

Back on the dorm roof, she transformed and slipped into the clothes she'd left there. Without Hatch's help, National would never have discovered the murderers. When the sheriff questioned them, the Ashton brothers had alibied each other. Without an obvious motive, there was no reason to follow up.

Marta must have suspected something, so she asked Tonya to investigate before she went to the authorities. With National's reputation for jumping to conclusions, Tonya didn't blame Marta for wanting to be sure. Her uncles weren't nice people, but they were family.

After National caught them red-handed trying to bury the murder weapon, Stephen and Marvin looked guilty, but Tonya still had to uncover their motive. Why had the Ashtons murdered their sister?

46

Early Monday morning, Tonya phoned Helen to tell her it was over. "National arrested Stephen and Marvin last night. They caught them digging a hole to hide the dragon claws."

Thanks to me, Hatch reminded her.

"I hope you're right, but National has a bad track record," Helen said. "Cases against the rich and connected don't always go to trial."

"I thought National's motto was 'guilty until proven innocent?'"

"That applies to ordinary people."

"There's no way I'll let Stephen or Marvin walk. If they get away with killing their own sister …"

"What can you do?" Helen asked.

"I'm going to figure out why they did it. Once the sheriff has means, motive, and the murder weapon they tried to hide, no amount of power or money will save them."

Sheriff Anderson told Tonya she couldn't be there when he questioned the Ashtons, but she promised new evidence to make them break. When she refused to reveal what she'd found over the phone, he let her sit in.

There was a new vibe when Tonya lifted the flap of the red pavilion and entered the interdimensional police station. Walking tall, she waved and smiled at the vampire detective and her Amazonian partner. They waved back! *How cool was that?*

When Runnymede, the turtle detective, rushed into the bullpen, he nodded to Tonya as he zipped by. Even the massive werewolf cop didn't rattle her anymore. With her new confidence, the stubble on his chin didn't make her nervous that he was going to transform into a ravenous beast. The extra chin hair looked hyper-masculine but handsome, and the way his eyes lingered on her didn't mean he wanted to eat her. Date her, maybe.

This isn't the time or place, Hatch reminded her.

I'm sorry. Does it make you uncomfortable when I think about guys?

Humans are yucky.

She was the first woman in history to share a body with a boy dragon. When he hit puberty, things would get awkward—but that was a future problem.

Anderson was waiting for her. "I put the Ashton brothers in separate rooms. We've started interviewing, but you've only missed the boring stuff."

Loon Lake's Old Families had their own laws and procedures, and they normally held trials at City Hall, where witch's advocates represented the accused. Since the 1800s, City Council updated and enforced the Old Family's strict rules. It was a peculiar way of doing things that stemmed from Loon Lake's desire to hide its magic.

National applied the same draconian laws in every jurisdiction, so you didn't call them in for cases requiring nuance. They assumed prisoners were guilty until proven innocent. Under normal circumstances, that idea would appall Tonya, but with the Ashton's money and clout, Helen had assured her they would get excellent lawyers and favorable treatment. Anderson would have to make a strong case.

"Let's start with Stephen." Anderson led Tonya down the hallway where he'd "questioned" Helen after the wake. Tonya faced a one-way mirror where she could watch and listen through the thin glass. "He's already lawyered up—probably because Marvin told him to."

Stephen wore designer overalls—the outfit he'd worn to bury the bones. He lounged in his chair, smirking. Seated next to Stephen was his handsome witch's advocate. He was tall and broad-shouldered with a blonde brush cut—as if Stephen had chosen the lawyer who looked most like his twin.

Dressed in a cobalt suit with contrasting peak lapels, the witch's advocate explained his client wouldn't speak or answer questions. Instead, they were co-operating with law enforcement by reading a prepared statement.

"When you found my client digging a hole, he was aiding the police. What you saw was an Ashton Security executive taking a hands-on approach to keeping our city safe. If National were half so conscientious, maybe your detectives would have caught the murderer by now instead of harassing the victim's grieving brother."

Anderson stood. "We apprehended Stephen hiding the murder weapon."

Stephen whispered in his advocate's ear.

"If you're not arresting my client ..." The advocate closed his briefcase. "He's tired and would like to go home."

Anderson rolled his eyes. "Yeah, he must be really worn out from fighting crime." The sheriff told Stephen he wasn't going anywhere and left the room.

In the hall, Tonya asked. "Do you have to let him go?"

"No. Let him stew in his own sweat while I question Marvin."

Tonya took her place behind a second two-way mirror, and Anderson switched on the camera. Marvin, who considered himself the smart one, sat alone without a witch's advocate.

Anderson got to the point. "Why were you digging a deep hole in the middle of the night?"

"I got hungry and went looking for turnips." Marvin didn't smirk like his brother, but his voice oozed superior attitude.

"I can charge you for murder based on your brother's testimony."

"We're innocent."

"Are you? It looked to me, and to the detectives on the scene, like you were burying evidence of a crime."

"I didn't do anything wrong."

"You just perjured yourself and obstructed justice with your lies." He pointed to the camera. "Turnips? No judge will believe that."

Marvin's smile wavered. "I'm waiting for my witch's advocate before I answer any more questions."

"Good. It's better for you to listen. Stephen says you met Donna on the beach and that you killed her with the claws."

"Nice try."

Tonya tapped on the glass. When Anderson came out, she whispered, "I don't think Marvin did it. What motive could he have? Donna was mayor, and she awarded big city contracts to their family business. He didn't hate Donna, and he loves money. His life is dedicated to spreadsheets. Do you really think he killed Ashton Security's biggest client in cold blood?"

"If Marvin thinks his brother is setting him up, he'll confess what he knows to save his skin."

"Only if he believes we know everything." As the words left her mouth, the pieces fell together for Tonya. The cool scent of the cologne. The infuriating crowds and protestors jamming up the streets of Loon Lake Village. "Let me speak to Stephen."

"He's not talking."

"I can make him."

Anderson led her into the room and took the seat beside her, across from Stephen and his advocate.

"Can I have a pad of paper?" she asked.

"Way ahead of you." Anderson set out a pen and pad of lined paper.

"What's she doing here?" Stephen asked.

"So much for his vow of silence." She winked at the witch's advocate. "Do you find your client has trouble with impulse control?"

The handsome counselor was too smart to rise to the bait, but Stephen stopped smiling and got out of his chair, paced a few steps, then sat back down.

"It must be hard being a spoiled brat," Tonya continued. "You get used to having everything your way all the time."

"She can't berate my client." The lawyer gave Anderson the side eye. "Get her out of here."

"National supports citizen involvement. The law shouldn't act behind closed doors."

"So let her watch quietly." The advocate's smooth neck and cheeks flushed.

Anderson told Tonya, "Ask whatever you like."

"That was genuine grief at your sister's funeral," she said. "You loved her, didn't you?"

"Yes." His voice was barely audible.

Tonya leaned across the table and sniffed. "Your cologne is cool and fresh, even after a sweaty night in a holding cell. It lasts because it's expensive."

"So?"

"I smelled the same fragrance on Donna's body." To Anderson she said, "And I'm willing to testify in court. So is Hatch."

In sync, she and Hatch composed the same thought. "What's wrong with you, Stephen?"

He cringed as if her words stung, while his advocate tried to shush him.

"Is your conscience bothering you?" Tonya kept up the attack. "Are you ashamed of screwing up again? Too scared to face what you've done?"

With his head in his hands, in a small voice, Stephen said, "Yes."

Tonya grinned. "Don't worry then. Your brother told us everything."

"What?"

"Oh, yeah. He won't go to jail for you. He asked for immunity and sold you out."

Stephen lunged at Tonya, who scraped her chair back just out of reach. Stephen's advocate made placating noises, but Stephen was beyond hearing. He swore and shouted, "I knew it! I'll kill him!"

Anderson whispered to Tonya, "Was there a purpose to this?"

"Absolutely." She asked Stephen to sit down. "You're going to feel a lot better once you come clean, so let me help you get started."

Stephen dropped into the chair, but when his advocate tried to speak, he waved him off.

"Life in Loon Lake Village is getting stressful," Tonya said. "With tourists flooding local shops and businesses, Mayor Ashton was supposed to fix things, but instead of once a week, the cruise ship started returning every day, turning your quiet village into chaos. Streets got so crowded, you couldn't drive your fancy sports cars in the Village."

Tonya paused for Stephen to add something. When he didn't, she continued. "Paloma and Roberto undercut the authority of Ashton Security and drained cash flow. They reduced Loon Lake Village to a theme park where Ashton Security was demoted to working the turnstiles. Their dragon, Flores, got the extra cash and admiration for patrolling the skies."

Stephen stared at the table.

"What happened?" She needed to his motive. "Where did it all go wrong?"

The advocate tried to silence him, but Stephen said, "It's okay. I want to tell her." Tears brightened his eyes, and he sniffled. "I'd been complaining to Donna for weeks about the noise, the disrespect. One tourist offered me a tip as if I was a waiter! And my sister, she never had any time for me. I told Donna to meet me at the Mod boathouse and tell me how she could end this, or I'd sell my share of the business and join the protesters myself."

Anderson made notes as Stephen continued. "On the way there, I must have stepped in a puddle of that slimy spell stuff. It's all over Loon Lake Village, but I didn't notice it until I was with Donna. The next minute we're arguing, and she's making excuses about contracts and red tape. Says she can't help me."

He swallowed. "Then I look down and the $2000.00 shoes I bought in Milan are smoking. The soles are melting. When my feet started burning, I lost it. I grabbed her neck and yelled and yelled. I didn't know I was shaking her until I felt something snap. Her face turned blue, and her heart stopped beating. It was an accident. I never meant to hurt her."

"Then what happened?" Tonya prodded.

"I panicked and called Marvin."

"Were the claws his idea?" Anderson asked.

Stephen nodded. "He ripped up my little sister's body." Face twisted in anguish, he hammered the table with his fist.

In time, he composed himself. "Send me to jail. I don't care, as long as you punish Marvin too."

"Does he need to write the confession," she asked Anderson, "or can we use the video?"

"Give me that paper." Stephen grabbed the pen. "I'm not illiterate."

47

It was New Year's Eve, and the police station had retreated to another dimension leaving the red pavilion behind. The interior was a natural size, and they had installed a polished wooden dance floor. Jars of glowing coffin-nosed moths hung from the crossbeams and snoozed contentedly, while here and there fireflies sparked at the edges of the pavilion like tiny living fireworks.

Colored lights hung from the tent poles strobing to Zain's upbeat playlist. The music thumped from big speakers Zain had connected to a laptop, leaving him and Grace free to dance nonstop. But as the clock wound down to midnight, even they came up for air.

Drake caught Tonya's eye.

Awkward, Tonya and Hatch thought in unison.

Drake closed the gap and held his arms open. "Hug?"

When she nodded, he gave her a light squeeze. "It's great to see you. I *love* the new hair."

Tonya was glad she'd gone light teal instead of blonde. "I'm happy to see you too."

Could she and Drake be just friends? They'd been buddies and Digital Ninjas together before they dated. Bottom line, she didn't want to lose someone who understood and accepted all her weirdness.

Hatch piped up, *Wait until he meets me.*

She chatted with Drake about his future film projects and plans for the holidays like they used to. The awkwardness was gone.

When he spotted his new girlfriend and left to meet her, she was happy for Drake.

Wow, Hatch enthused, *I think humans call that wearing your big girl pants.*

From the ceiling, a burst of glitter erupted, tickling Tonya's arms and making Hatch giggle. The music slowed, and Grace led Zain back to the dance floor for a close-up clinch. Drake followed with his girl.

Not in the mood to find a partner, Tonya searched out her best friend for a chat. At the bar, Priya commanded attention with her regal posture. She wore silver sandals and a shimmery black dress that captivated a handful of handsome National police rookies gathered around her.

Maybe not such a good time to bother Priya. Tonya backtracked to the snack table and ladled herself a glass of punch.

"I'm happy your friends came to the party." Anderson held a shortbread cookie in one hand and a glass of champagne in the other.

"Thanks for inviting us."

"Might as well use the pavilion. We can throw as much confetti as we like, and there's no cleanup. The whole thing disappears in the morning."

"You're sweet to think of us, but tell me, what happens to Stephen and Marvin now?"

"They'll be tried, found guilty on your evidence, and then shipped off to National prison."

"Will Marta be able to visit her brothers?"

"Marvin might make it back someday, if they shorten his sentence for good behavior."

"But Stephen?"

Anderson shook his head. "You'll never see him again."

If National hadn't stepped in, the Old Families would have given Stephen and Marvin a terminal sentence. Practitioners were too powerful to get second chances.

"What about Flores?"

"None of this was her fault."

"Don't play dumb. She's an intelligent creature exploited by the Alvarez family. Are you taking up her case with National?"

"If it's that important to you, I will."

Good. I'll keep you to that, Hatch's words rung in their heads.

Anderson put down his drink and led her away from the table. "I want to talk to you about something else."

Oh no. They had gotten too close with their dragon-to-dragon telepathy, but that's all it was to Tonya, friendly communication. She braced herself to rebuff the older man without hurting his feelings.

"I have an offer for you, but first I want to be sure there aren't any personal feelings between us."

"Personal like what?"

"I was impressed by how you found Donna's killer, and before that how you proved Helen's innocence. It's tough to go against National."

"She was going to die. I'd do anything to save Mom."

He whispered, "And she's done *plenty* for National, but that's finished now."

Wow. Her mother, the former spy.

"But let's talk about you. There's a place for you at the National Police Academy."

Her heart raced. "What about my studies here?"

"Would you miss the university?"

"No, but what if I hurt somebody with my magic? Until it's under control, I'm a menace. And my friends ..." Tonya would miss them if she left, except their tight little group wouldn't last. She'd lost a year of school to illness. After next year they would graduate, leaving her to complete her degree alone.

"How can I control my magic if I drop out of university?"

"The Academy will train you to be a lethal weapon—one that never goes off by accident. What do you say?"

"I'm in."

"And the personal feelings stuff?"

"I'll try not to hold them against you."

He toasted her with his shortbread cookie. "See you after you graduate from the Academy."

For free stories and publishing updates visit maajawentz.com

Loon Lake Magic Series

by Maaja Wentz

Feeding Frenzy: Curse of the Necromancer
Double Dead Magic
Witch Gone Dragon

Find this series and more at:
books2read.com/maajawentz

About the Author

Maaja Wentz is an award-winning writer of fantasy and mystery stories. Her short mystery, "Inside of a Dog," is available as a free ebook at maajawentz.com. It first appeared in *Ellery Queen Mystery Magazine* which called it "very original."

To hear about upcoming publications and get free stories, join the Loon Lake reading club at maajawentz.com.

For my uncles Ralph, Doug, and Larry.